The Germ Growers

An Australian story of adventure and mystery

Robert Potter

The Germ Growers: An Australian story of adventure and mystery

ISBN: 978-1-64799-364-1

TABLE OF CONTENTS

PRELIMINARY

When I first heard the name of Kimberley[1] it did not remind me of the strange things which I have here to record, and which I had witnessed somewhere in its neighbourhood years before. But one day, in the end of last summer, I overheard a conversation about its geography which led me to recognise it as a place that I had formerly visited under very extraordinary circumstances. The recognition was in this wise. Jack Wilbraham and I were spending a little while at a hotel in Gippsland, partly on a tour of pleasure and partly, so at least we persuaded ourselves, on business. The fact was, however, that for some days past, the business had quite retreated into the background, or, to speak more correctly, we had left it behind at Bairnsdale, and had come in search of pleasure a little farther south.

It was delicious weather, warm enough for light silk coats in the daytime, and cold enough for two pairs of blankets at night. We had riding and sea-bathing to our hearts' content, and even a rough kind of yachting and fishing. The ocean was before us—we heard its thunder night and day; and the lakes were behind us, stretching away to the promontory which the Mitchell cuts in two, and thence to the mouth of the Latrobe, which is the highway to Sale. Three times a week a coach passed our door, bound for the Snowy River and the more savage regions beyond. Any day for a few shillings we could be driven to Lake Tyers, to spend a day amidst scenery almost comparable with the incomparable Hawkesbury. Last of all, if we grew tired of the bell-birds and the gum-trees and the roar of the ocean, we were within a day's journey of Melbourne by lake and river and rail.

It was our custom to be out all day, but home early and early to bed. We used to take our meals in a low long room which was well aired but poorly lighted, whether by day or night. And here, when tea was over and the womenkind had retired, we smoked, whenever, as often happened, the evening was cold enough to make a shelter desirable; smoked and chatted. There was light enough to see the smoke of your pipe and the faces of those near you; but if you were listening to the chatter of a group in the other end of the room the faces of the speakers were so indistinct as often to give a startling challenge to your imagination if you had one, and if it was

---

[1] In North-west Australia.

accustomed to take the bit in its teeth. I sometimes caught myself partly listening to a story-teller in the other end of the room and partly fashioning a face out of his dimly seen features, which quite belied the honest fellow's real countenance when the flash of a pipelight or a shifted lamp revealed it more fully.

Jack and I were more of listeners than talkers, and we were usually amongst the earliest who retired. But one evening there was a good deal of talk about the new gold-field in the north-west, and a keen-looking bushman who seemed to have just returned from the place began to describe its whereabouts. Then I listened attentively, and at one point in his talk, I started and looked over at Jack, and I saw that he was already looking at me. I got up and left the room without a sign to him, but I knew that he would follow me, and he did. It was bright moonlight, and when we met outside we strolled down to the beach together. It was a wide, long, and lonely beach, lonely to the very last degree, and it was divided from the house by a belt of scrub near a mile wide. We said not a word to one another till we got quite near the sea. Then I turned round and looked Jack in the face and said, "Why, man, it must have been quite near the place."

"No," said he, "it may have been fifty miles or more away, their knowledge is loose, and their description looser, but it must be somewhere in the neighbourhood, and I suppose they are sure to find it."

"I do not know," said I; and after a pause I added, "Jack, it seems to me they might pass all over the place and see nothing of what we saw."

"God knows," he muttered, and then he sat down on a hummock of sand and I beside him. Then he said, "Why have you never told the story, Bob?"

"Don't you know why, Jack?" I answered. "They would lock me up in a madhouse; there would be no one to corroborate me but you, and if you did so you would be locked up along with me."

"That might be," said he, "if they believed you; but they would not believe you, they would think you were simply romancing."

"What would be the good of speaking then?" said I.

"Don't speak," he repeated, "but write, litera scripta manet, you will be believed sometime. But meanwhile you can take as your motto that verse in Virgil about the gate of ivory, and that will save you from being thought mad. You have a knack of the pen, Bob, you ought to try it."

"Well," said I, "let it be a joint concern between you and me, and I'll do my best."

v

Then we lit our pipes and walked home, and settled the matter in a very few words on the way. I was to write, but all I should write was to be read over to Jack, who should correct and supplement it from his own memory. And no account of anything which was witnessed by both of us was to stand finally unless it was fully vouched for by the memory of both. Thus for any part of the narrative which would concern one of us only that one should be alone responsible, but for all of it in which we were both concerned there should be a joint responsibility.

Out of this agreement comes the following history, and thus it happens that it is told in the first person singular, although there are two names on the title-page.

CHAPTER I

DISAPPEARANCES

Before I begin my story I must give you some account of certain passages in my early life, which seem to have some connection with the extraordinary facts that I am about to put on record.

To speak more precisely, of the connection of one of them with those facts there can be no doubt at all, and of the connection of the other with them I at least have none.

When I was quite a boy, scarce yet fifteen years old, I happened to be living in a parish on the Welsh coast, which I will here call Penruddock. There were some bold hills inland and some very wild and rugged cliffs along the coast. But there was also a well-sheltered beach and a little pier where some small fishing vessels often lay. Penruddock was not yet reached by rail, but forty miles of a splendid road, through very fine scenery, took you to a railway station. And this journey was made by a well-appointed coach on five days of every week.

The people of Penruddock were very full of a queer kind of gossip, and were very superstitious. And I took the greatest interest in their stories. I cannot say that I really believed them, or that they affected me with any real fear. But I was not without that mingled thrill of doubt and wonder which helps one to enjoy such things. I had a double advantage in this way, for I could understand the Welsh language, although I spoke it but little and with difficulty, and I often found a startling family likeness between the stories which I heard in the cottages of the peasantry three or four miles out of town and those which circulated among the English-speaking people in whose village I lived.

There was one such story which was constantly reproduced under various forms. Sometimes it was said to have happened in the last generation; sometimes as far back as the civil wars, of which, strange to say, a lively traditional recollection still remained in the neighbourhood; and sometimes it seemed to have been handed down from prehistoric times, and was associated with tales of enchantment and fairyland. In such stories the central event was always the unaccountable disappearance of some person, and the character of the person disappearing always presented certain

1

unvarying features. He was always bold and fascinating, and yet in some way or other very repulsive. And when you tried to find out why, some sort of inhumanity was always indicated, some unconscious lack of sympathy which was revolting in a high degree or even monstrous. The stories had one other feature in common, of which I will tell you presently.

I seldom had any companions of my own age, and I was in consequence more given to dreaming than was good for me. And I used to marshal the heroes of these queer stories in my day-dreams and trace their likeness one to another. They were often so very unlike in other points, and yet so strangely like in that one point. I remember very well the first day that I thought I detected in a living man a resemblance to those dreadful heroes of my Welsh friend's folk-lore. There was a young fellow whom I knew, about five or six years my senior, and so just growing into manhood. His name, let us say, was James Redpath. He was well built, of middle height, and, as I thought, at first at least, quite beautiful to look upon. And, indeed, why I did not continue to think so is more than I can exactly say. For he possessed very fine and striking features, and although not very tall his presence was imposing. But nobody liked him. The girls especially, although he was so good-looking, almost uniformly shrank from him. But I must confess that he did not seem to care much for their society.

I went about with him a good deal at one time on fishing and shooting excursions and made myself useful to him, and except that he was rather cruel to dogs and cats, and had a nasty habit of frightening children, I do not know that I noticed anything particular about him. Not, at least, until one day of which I am going to tell you. James Redpath and I were coming back together to Penruddock, and we called at a cottage about two miles from the village. Here we found a little boy of about four years old, who had been visiting at the cottage and whom they wanted to send home. They asked us to take charge of him and we did so. On the way home the little boy's shoe was found to have a nail or a peg in it that hurt his foot, and we were quite unable to get it out. It was nothing, however, to James Redpath to carry him, and so he took him in his arms. The little boy shrank and whimpered as he did so. James had under his arm some parts of a fishing-rod and one of these came in contact with the little boy's leg and scratched it rather severely so as to make him cry. I took it away and we went on. I was walking a little behind Redpath, and as I walked I saw him deliberately take another joint of the rod, put it in the same place and then watch the little boy's face as it came in contact with the wire, and as the child

2

cried out I saw quite a malignant expression of pleasure pass over James's face. The thing was done in a moment and it was over in a moment; but I felt as if I should like to have killed him if I dared. I always dreaded and shunned him, more or less, afterwards, and I began from that date to associate him with the inhuman heroes of my Welsh stories.

I don't think that I should ever have got over the dislike of him which I then conceived, but I saw the last of him, at least Penruddock saw the last of him, about three months later. I had been sitting looking over the sea between the pier and the cliffs and trying to catch a glimpse of the Wicklow Mountains which were sometimes to be seen from that point. Just then James Redpath came up from the beach beyond the pier, and passing me with a brief "good morning," went away inland, leaving the cliffs behind him. I don't know how long I lay there, it might be two hours or more, and I think I slept a little. But I suddenly started up to find it high day and past noon, and I began to think of looking for some shelter. There was not a cloud visible, but nevertheless two shadows like, or something like, the shadows of clouds lay near me on the ground. What they were the shadows of I could not tell, and I was about to get up to see, for there was nothing to cast such a shadow within the range of my sight as I lay. Just then one of the shadows came down over me and seemed to stand for a moment between me and the sun. It had a well-defined shape, much too well defined for a cloud. I thought as I looked that it was just such a shadow as might be cast by a yawl-built boat lying on the body of a large wheelbarrow. Then the two shadows seemed to move together and to move very quickly. I had just noticed that they were exactly like one another when the next moment they passed out of my sight.

I started to my feet with a bound, my heart beating furiously. But there was nothing more to alarm the weakest. It was broad day. Houses and gardens were to be seen close at hand and in every direction but one, and in that direction there were three or four fishermen drawing their nets. But as I looked away to the part of the sky where the strange cloudlike shadows had just vanished, I remembered with a shudder that other feature in common of the strange stories of which I told you just now. It was a feature that forcibly reminded me of what I had just witnessed. Sometimes in the later stories you would be told of a cloud coming and going in an otherwise cloudless sky. And sometimes in the elder stories you would be told of an invisible car, invisible but not shadowless. I used always to identify the shadow of the invisible car in the elder stories with the cloud in the later stories, the cloud that unaccountably came and went.

3

As I thought it all over and tried to persuade myself that I had been dreaming I suddenly remembered that James Redpath had passed by a few hours before, and as suddenly I came to the conclusion that I should never see him again. And certainly he never was again seen, dead or alive, anywhere in Wales or England. His father, and his uncle, and their families, continued to live about Penruddock, but Penruddock never knew James Redpath any more. Whether I myself saw him again or not is more than I can say with absolute certainty. You shall know as much as I know about it if you hear my story to the end.

4

CHAPTER II

THE RED SICKNESS

Of course James Redpath's disappearance attracted much attention, and was the talk not only of the village, but of the whole country-side. It was the general opinion that he must have been drowned by falling over the cliffs, and that his body had been washed out to sea. I proved, however, to have been the very last person to see him, and my testimony, as far as it went, was against that opinion. For I certainly had seen him walking straight inland. Of course he might have returned to the coast afterwards, but at least nobody had seen him return. I gave a full account of place and time as far as I could fix them, and I mentioned the queer-looking clouds and even described their shape. This, I remember, was considered to have some value as fixing my memory of the matter, but no further notice was taken of it. And I myself did not venture to suggest any connection between it and Redpath's disappearance, because I did not see how I could reasonably do so. I had, nevertheless, a firm conviction that there was such a connection, but I knew very well that to declare it would only bring a storm of ridicule upon me.

But a public calamity just then befell Penruddock which made men forget James Redpath's disappearance. A pestilence broke out in the place of which nobody knew either the nature or the source. It seemed to spring up in the place. At least, all efforts to trace it were unsuccessful. The first two or three cases were attributed to some inflammatory cold, but it soon became clear that there were specific features about it, that they were quite unfamiliar, that the disease was extremely dangerous to life and highly infectious.

Then a panic set in, and I believe that the disease would soon have been propagated all over England and farther, if it had not been for the zeal and ability of two young physicians who happened very fortunately to be living in the village just then. Their names were Leopold and Furniss. I forget if I ever knew their Christian names. We used to call them Doctor Leopold and Doctor Furniss. They had finished their studies for some little time, but they found it advisable on the score of health to take a longish holiday before commencing practice, and they were spending part of their holiday at Penruddock. They were just about to leave us when the disease I am telling you of broke out.

5

The first case occurred in a valley about two miles from the village. In this valley there were several cottages inhabited mostly by farm labourers and artisans. These cottages lay one after another in the direction of the rising ground which separated the valley from Penruddock. Then there were no houses for a considerable space. Then, just over the hill, there was another and yet another. The disease had made its way gradually up the hill from one cottage to another, day after day a fresh case appearing. Then there had been no new cases for four days, but on the fifth day a new case appeared in the cottage just over the brow of the hill. And when this became known, also that every case (there had now been eleven) had hitherto been fatal, serious alarm arose. Then, too, the disease became known as the "red sickness." This name was due to a discoloration which set in on the shoulders, neck, and forehead very shortly after seizure.

How the two doctors, as we called them, became armed with the needful powers I do not know. They certainly contrived to obtain some sort of legal authority, but I think that they acted in great measure on their own responsibility.

By the time they commenced operations there were three or four more cases in the valley, and one more in the second cottage on the Penruddock side. There was a large stone house, partly ruinous, in the valley, near the sea, and hither they brought every one of the sick. Plenty of help was given them in the way of beds, bedding, and all sorts of material, but such was the height which the panic had now attained that no one from the village would go near any of the sick folk, nor even enter the valley. The physicians themselves and their two men servants, who seemed to be as fearless and brave as they, did all the work. Fortunately, the two infected cottages on the Penruddock side were each tenanted only by the person who had fallen ill, and the tenant in each case was a labourer whose work lay in the valley. The physicians burnt down these cottages and everything that was in them. Then they established a strict quarantine between the village and the valley. There was a light fence running from the sea for about a mile inland, along the brow of the rising ground on the Penruddock side. This they never passed nor suffered any one to pass, during the prevalence of the sickness. Butchers and bakers and other tradesmen left their wares at a given point at a given time, and the people from the valley came and fetched them.

The excitement and terror in Penruddock were very great. All but the most necessary business was suspended, and of social intercourse during the panic there was next to none. Ten cases in all

6

were treated by the physicians, and four of these recovered. The last two cases were three or four days apart, but they were no less malignant in character: the very last case was one of the fatal ones. I learned nothing of the treatment; but the means used to prevent the disease spreading, besides the strict quarantine, were chiefly fire and lime. Everything about the sick was passed through the fire, and of these everything that the fire would destroy was destroyed. Lime, which abounded in the valley, was largely used.

A month after the last case the two physicians declared the quarantine at an end, and a month later all fear of the disease had ceased. And then the people of the village began to think of consoling themselves for the dull and uncomfortable time they had had, and of doing some honour to the two visitors who had served the village so well. With this double purpose in view a picnic on a large scale was organized, and there was plenty of eating and drinking and speech-making and dancing, all of which I pass over. But at that picnic I heard a conversation which made a very powerful impression on me then, and which often has seemed to provide a bond which binds together all the strange things of which I had experience at the time and afterwards.

In the heat of the afternoon I had happened to be with Mr. Leopold and Mr. Furniss helping them in some arrangements which they were making for the amusement of the children who took part in the picnic. After these were finished they two strolled away together to the side of a brook which ran through the park where we were gathered. I followed them, attracted mainly by Mr. Furniss's dog, but encouraged also by an occasional word from the young men. At the brook Mr. Furniss sat upon a log, and leaned his back against a rustic fence. The dog sat by him; a very beautiful dog he was, black and white, with great intelligent eyes, and an uncommonly large and well-shaped head. He would sometimes stretch himself at length, and then again he would put his paw upon his master's shoulder and watch Mr. Leopold and me.

Mr. Leopold stood with his back to an oak-tree, and I leant against the fence beside him listening to him. He was a tall, dark man, with a keen, thoughtful, and benevolent expression. He was quite strong and healthy-looking, and there was a squareness about his features that I think one does not often see in dark people. Mr. Furniss was of lighter complexion and hardly as tall; there was quite as much intelligence and benevolence in his face, but not so much of what I have called thoughtfulness as distinguished from intelligence, and there was a humorous glint in his eye which the other lacked. They began to talk about the disease which had been so successfully dealt with, and this was what they said:—

7

Leopold. Well, Furniss, an enemy hath done this.

Furniss. Done what? The picnic or the red sickness?

Leopold. The red sickness, of course. Can't you see what I mean?

Furniss. No, I can't. You're too much of a mystic for me, Leopold; but I'll tell you what, England owes a debt to you and me, my boy, for it was near enough to being a new edition of the black death or the plague.

Leopold. Only the black death and the plague were imported, and this was indigenous. It sprung up under our noses in a healthy place. It came from nowhere, and, thank God, it is gone nowhither.

Furniss. But surely the black death and the plague must have begun somewhere, and they too seem to have gone nowhither.

Leopold. You're right this far that they all must have had the same sort of beginning. Only it is given to very few to see the beginning, as you and I have seen it, or so near the beginning.

Furniss. Now, Leopold, I hardly see what you are driving at. I am not much on religion, as they say in America, but I believe there is a Power above all. Call that Power God, and let us say that God does as He pleases, and on the whole that it is best that He should. I don't see that you can get much further than that.

Leopold. I don't believe that God ever made the plague, or the black death, or the red sickness.

Furniss. Oh, don't you? Then you are, I suppose, what the churchmen call a Manichee—you believe in the two powers of light and darkness, good and evil. Well, it is not a bad solution of the question as far as it goes, but I can hardly accept it.

Leopold. No, I don't believe in any gods but the One. But let me explain. That is a nice dog of yours, Furniss. You told me one day something about his breeding, and you promised to tell me more.

Furniss. Yes, it is quite a problem in natural history. Do you know, Tommy's ancestors have been in our family for four or five generations of men, and, I suppose, that is twenty generations of dogs.

Leopold. You told me something of it. You improved the breed greatly, I believe?

Furniss. Yes; but I have some distant cousins, and they have the same breed and yet not the same, for they have cultivated it in quite another direction.

Leopold. What are the differences?

Furniss. Our dogs are all more or less like Tommy here, gentle and faithful, very intelligent, and by no means deficient in pluck. My

8

cousin's dogs are fierce and quarrelsome, so much so that they have not been suffered for generations to associate with children. And so they have lost intelligence and are become ill-conditioned and low-lived brutes.

Leopold. But I think I understood you to say that the change in the breed did not come about in the ordinary course of nature.

Furniss. I believe not. I heard my grandfather say that his father had told him that when he was a young man he had set about improving the breed. He had marked out the most intelligent and best tempered pups, and he had bred from them only and had given away or destroyed the others.

Leopold. And about your cousin's dogs?

Furniss. Just let me finish. It seems that while one brother began to cultivate the breed upward, so to speak, another brother was living in a part of the country where thieves were numerous and daring, and there were smugglers and gipsies, and what not, about. And so he began to improve the breed in quite another direction. He selected the fierce and snappish pups and bred exclusively from them.

Leopold. And so from one ancestral pair of, say, a hundred or a hundred and fifty years ago, you have Tommy there, with his wonderful mixture of gentleness and pluck, and his intelligence all but human, and your cousin has a kennel of unintelligent and bloodthirsty brutes, that have to be caged and chained as if they were wild beasts.

Furniss. Just so, but I don't quite see what you are driving at.

Leopold. Wait a minute. Do you suppose the germs of cow-pox and small-pox to be of the same breed?

Furniss. Well, yes; you know that I hold them to be specifically identical. I see what you are at now.

Leopold. But one of them fulfils some obscure function in the physique of the cow, some function certainly harmless and probably beneficent, and the other is the malignant small-pox of the London hospitals.

Furniss. So you mean to infer that in the latter case the germ has been cultivated downwards by intelligent purpose.

Leopold. What if I do?

Furniss. You think, then, that there is a secret guild of malignant men of medicine sworn to wage war against their fellow-men, that they are spread over all the world and have existed since before the dawn of history. I don't believe that there are any men as bad as that, and if there were, I should call them devils and hunt them down like mad dogs.

9

Leopold. I don't wish to use misleading words, but I will say that I believe there are intelligences, not human, who have access to realms of nature that we are but just beginning to explore; and I believe that some of them are enemies to humanity, and that they use their knowledge to breed such things as malignant small-pox or the red sickness out of germs which were originally of a harmless or even of a beneficent nature.

Furniss. Just as my cousins have bred those wild beasts of theirs out of such harmless creatures as poor Tommy's ancestors.

Leopold. Just so.

Furniss. And you think that we can contend successfully against such enemies.

Leopold. Why not? They can only have nature to work upon. And very likely their only advantage over us is that they know more of nature than we do. They cannot go beyond the limits of nature to do less or more. As long as we sought after spells and enchantments and that sort of nonsense we were very much at their mercy. But we are now learning to fight them with their own weapons, which consist of the knowledge of nature. Witness vaccination, and witness also our little victory over the red sickness.

Furniss. You're a queer mixture, Leopold, but we must get back to the picnic people.

And so they got up and went back together to the dancers, nodding to me as they went. I sat there for awhile, going over and over the conversation in my mind and putting together my own thoughts and Mr. Leopold's.

Then I joined the company and was merry as the merriest for the remainder of the day. But that night I dreamt of strange-looking clouds and of the shadows of invisible cars, and of demons riding in the cars and sowing the seeds of pestilence on the earth and catching away such evil specimens of humanity as James Redpath to reinforce the ranks of their own malignant order.

CHAPTER III

AT SEA

It is my purpose to pass briefly over everything in my own history which does not concern the tale that I have to tell, and there is very little therefore for me to say about the seven or eight years which followed upon the events at Penruddock which I have just recorded.

I went in due course to Oxford, where I stayed the usual time. I did not make any great failures there, nor did I gain much distinction. I was a diligent reader, but much of my reading was outside the regulation lines. The literature of my own country, the poetry of mediæval Italy, and the philosophy of modern Germany, more than divided my attention with classics and mathematics. Novels, mostly of the sensational type, amused me in vacations and on holidays, but very seldom found their way into my working days.

I travelled over most of England, Scotland, and Ireland, and spent some time in some of the principal cities of the Continent. I became a fair linguist, speaking German, French, and Italian, with some fluency, although my accent always bewrayed me. I took a second class in classics, bade adieu to Oxford, and began to make up my mind as to what I should do with my life. I had thought of the various professions in turn, and had decided against them all; and, finally, as I had no taste for idleness, and as I had some money, I resolved to invest it in sheep or cattle farming in some of the new countries. I thought successively of New Zealand, the United States, Canada, and Australia, and I was determined in favour of Australia by falling in with Jack Wilbraham. He and I had gone into residence at Oxford about the same time, but not at the same college, and we took our degrees in the same year; but we hardly belonged to the same set. Jack was more of a sporting than a reading man, and I was not much of either, at least as either was understood at the University. So Jack and I, although we heard of one another occasionally, did not meet until a few months before we left Oxford.

Then we became fast friends, and, as he had already determined to go to Australia, I made up my mind to go with him. We took our passage of course in the same ship. It was not yet the day of the great steamers and the canal was not yet open. We sailed from Liverpool in a clipper ship and we went round the Cape. But I

11

think that we were quite as comfortable and as well taken care of as we should be now in the best of the Orient or Peninsular boats. Our voyage was altogether without disaster. Indeed it was like a picnic of ninety days' duration, and I do not know that I had ever enjoyed any three months of my life as much. But there were no details that I need mention except the fact that we formed an acquaintance (Jack and I) which determined our immediate course on our arrival in Australia, and so led us on to the mysterious experience of which I have to tell.

Not indeed that our new acquaintance was one who might fairly be expected to introduce us to anything mysterious. Mr. Fetherston, as I shall call him here, was a thoroughly good fellow, and proved himself to be a staunch friend, but he was utterly destitute of imagination, and he had the greatest contempt for what he used to call "queer stories"; he used queer in a special sense; he meant simply mysterious, or savouring of what is commonly called the supernatural.

One bright evening in the tropics some such stories were going round. The air was delicious, and the moon and stars were just beginning to shine. The first mate, myself, and Mr. Fetherston were the principal talkers, but we had a good many listeners. The first mate began the conversation by telling two or three stories of the type I have mentioned; one of them especially took my fancy. I cannot remember it in detail, but I know that it was provokingly mysterious, and seemed to admit of no solution but a supernatural one. The main incident was something like this. A farmer who lived about twelve miles from Bristol left home one evening with the intention of spending the night in that city in order to transact some business there at an early hour in the morning. He had to stop at a station about half-way to see some one who lived near there, and then to take another train in. He got out all right at the half-way station and walked towards the man's house whom he wanted to see. A stranger met him on the way and drew him into conversation. As they came to certain cross roads the stranger turned, looked him in the face and said very deliberately, "Go home by next train, you will be just in time." Then he walked away quickly down one of the cross roads. The farmer stood like one stunned for a minute or two, and then hurried after the stranger intending to stop him. But he could see him no more. There were several houses and gardens about and he might have passed into one of them, but anyhow he was lost to sight. The farmer did as he was told and hurried home. He arrived just in time to save his house from being burned to the ground, and more than that, for his wife and children and servants were in bed and asleep.

When the story was told, Mr. Fetherston gave his opinion of it very freely. I never saw contempt more effectually expressed. He spoke without the least atom of temper. Men who get angry and denounce that sort of thing are usually afraid of believing it, or at least of seeming to believe it. Nothing was further from Mr. Fetherston's thought. But you saw plainly that such stories were for him on a level with the most senseless of nursery rhymes and nothing better than mere idiot's chatter. He did not say so in as many words nor at all offensively, but he made it quite clear nevertheless that he felt himself to be looking down from the platform of a mysterious intelligence on some very contemptible folly.

I felt as if reproach were in the air, and I knew that if it were deserved I was one of those who deserved it. So, although it would have been pleasanter to be silent, I felt that I was bound to speak.

So I said, "Mr. Fetherston, isn't it all a matter of evidence?"

Fetherston. Evidence! And pray on what evidence would you believe such a story as that which we have just heard?

Easterley. Upon the statement on the honour of any sane man that I knew and trusted: how I might account for it is another matter.

Fetherston. If a man whom I knew and trusted told me such a story on his honour I should trust him no longer, and I should believe him to be either insane or dishonest.

Easterley. Suppose that ten men whom you knew and trusted agreed in telling you the same story?

Fetherston (with a slight laugh). Then I should begin to suspect that I had gone mad myself, but I should never believe it.

Easterley. Yet you believe a story which is nearly two thousand years old and which is full of mystery from beginning to end: the story of a man who was born mysteriously, who exercised mysterious powers during his life, and after death by violence lived again mysteriously, and at last left this world mysteriously. [Now you must know I spoke here knowing what I was about, for Fetherston was an enthusiastic churchman, and in company with a clergyman who was one of us he had organized a regular Sunday service, and, on the very last Sunday, was one of a small number to whom the clergyman had administered the sacrament.] It seems to me, Mr. Fetherston, I went on to say, that you, like some people I have met, can believe a thing with one side of your head and disbelieve it with the other.

13

Fetherston. You are certainly like some people I have met. You throw the Christian religion overboard and then you take to believing a lot of puerile absurdities.

Easterley. Softly now, you must not say that I throw the Christian religion overboard. It may be that I do not accept it in quite the same sense as you, still I accept it. And as for the supernatural, if I said that I believed in it or that I did not believe in it, I should most likely to some extent deceive you.

Fetherston. You mean that you could not answer with a plain "yes" or "no."

Easterley. Not quite that; but I could not answer as you do with "yes" and "no." I should have to distinguish.

Fetherston. Distinguish then, please.

Easterley. Well, when you say that you don't believe in the supernatural, I reply that what I don't believe in is the natural.

Fetherston. I am afraid I must ask you to explain your explanation.

Easterley. What I mean is this. I believe that there is nothing at all, from a bucket of saltwater to the head on your shoulders, of which a full account can be given by any man. You go further and further back until you can get no further, but still you see that you are not at the end. Every natural thing implies a principle which is outside nature.

Fetherston. But you believe that there is a law for everything?

Easterley. I believe that order prevails everywhere, and that everything has its place in that order; you may if you like call that order nature. Then I say that if there be ghosts they are part of nature; they have their place in nature as well as we. And we as well as the ghosts, and the air and the water as well as we, imply something that is not nature. Everything is natural and everything is supernatural.

Fetherston. Easterley, I am afraid you are a philosopher. Come with me to Central Australia and we'll knock the philosophy out of you and make you a practical man.

Easterley. Are you going to Central Australia?

Fetherston. Yes; I am to have charge of a company of surveyors who are to be engaged about the laying of the overland line to Port Darwin.

Easterley. I'll think of it. I rather think I should like it. I suppose we shall see no ghosts there, Fetherston?

Fetherston. I don't know about that. I dare say we may, for we shall often have to live on salt junk and damper.

So there our talk ended. I had heard of Mr. Fetherston's business before, and even I believe of his destination; but I had forgotten the particulars, and certainly it never had struck me that I should care to go with him. But now I thought I should like to talk it over with Jack. So I went in search of him. I found him by himself at the farthest aft part of the ship, standing just above the companion with his back against a rail. He had been chatting with two or three of the ladies, and they had just gone below. He came at once to meet me, and we both went forward and lit our pipes and smoked some time in silence. Then Jack spoke. "I see that you have something to say, Bob; what is it?"

"Fetherston," said I, "is going with a survey party to assist in laying the overland wire to Port Darwin: he proposes that we should go with him; he was only in jest, but I think I should like it."

Jack thought it would be a very good beginning: we should see much of the country, we should get experience, and have something to talk about. Poor Jack! if he had only known! We have never ventured to talk much about that journey, not much to one another, and not at all to anyone else; but I must not anticipate. We both took a fancy to the scheme. There would be much of the interest of exploring without any of the special risks. We would, no doubt, have some hardships to put up with, but there would be depôts at intervals along the way, and our communication would be kept open all through. So I spoke to Fetherston a few days later. "Fetherston," I said, "will you take two volunteers with you on your survey party northward? We shall pay our own expenses, but we shall want your guidance and protection, and we shall have nothing to give you in return but our company."

Fetherston said that he thought it might on such terms be easily managed, and it was managed accordingly.

CHAPTER IV

OVERLAND

Jack and I had intended to go on to Melbourne and thence to Sydney, but upon our arrival at Adelaide we found that arrangements had been made which required that Mr. Fetherston should start northward as soon as possible. We had, therefore, little enough time to make preparation for the journey, and so we had to give up for the present all thought of making acquaintance with the great Australian cities. Mr. Fetherston, although he was but little over thirty years old, was a veteran Australian explorer; for about ten years before he had been with Stuart on his third and successful expedition in search of a practicable route from Adelaide to the Indian Ocean, and all the time since, except about a year and a half in England and on the way there and back, he had spent in pioneering work in Queensland and the north.

The undertaking in which he was now engaged was in rather a critical condition. The entire length of the route, from Adelaide to Port Darwin, would be about two thousand miles, and over the central section of eight hundred miles, passing through, as some would have thought, the most difficult part of the line, the wire had been already carried. And after some further delay this had been connected with Adelaide. But about six hundred miles at the northern extremity still remained unfinished. The first expedition for the purpose had absolutely failed, and one or two attempts made since had not been any more successful. The chief superintendent of the work was either about to start for Port Darwin by sea, or was already on his way. And Mr. Fetherston's expedition was to meet him in the north. They expected to hear of one another somewhere about the Daly Waters. So there would be no work but simply travelling until that point was reached; none, at least, for Mr. Fetherston's party.

Mr. Fetherston introduced us to his chief assistant, Mr. Berry, telling us that we could do no better than take his advice about our preparation for the journey. Mr. Berry was also a veteran bushman and an experienced surveyor. He had been to Cooper's Creek twice, and he knew the Darling from Bourke to Wentworth as well as King William Street and the North Terrace. So Jack and I put ourselves into his hands. We purchased two strong saddle horses, each with

16

colonial saddles of the sort used by stockmen, and everything to match. We hired a man, specially recommended as a good bushman by Mr. Berry. This man was to ride one horse and to lead another, so that we should have one spare horse in case of accident. Mr. Fetherston introduced us also to the department which had oversight of the work. And they allowed us to pay a bulk sum to cover our expenses on the journey. The sum seemed to me very moderate, but, as Mr. Berry explained, "it was only to cover tucker and tents;" and the former was to be of a very simple and primitive sort, consisting simply of tea and sugar, salt meat and flour, and lime-juice, and we were to manage our cooking the best way we could. The store waggons would carry tobacco and soap; but these were to be sold, and Mr. Berry advised us to take a private supply of the former. We also procured a revolver each, and as many cartridges as we could conveniently carry. We each provided ourselves with a pair of blankets, an opossum rug, a couple of changes of coarse outside clothing, and half-a-dozen flannel shirts. Our dressing gear was limited to a comb and a tooth-brush each, with a few coarse towels. The towels and shirts we hoped to be able to wash from time to time on the way, and Mr. Berry told us that at depôts along the line there would sometimes be a supply of flannel shirts, and moleskin trousers, and cabbage-tree hats. The cabbage-tree hat was the head gear that we adopted by his advice.

Before leaving Adelaide we put our money in the bank, arranging that it should bear interest at some low rate for six months, and then we made our wills, which we left in the safe belonging to the bank. By Mr. Fetherston's advice we took very little money with us. A few sovereigns and some silver, he said, would be more than enough. Whatever we might buy at the Government depôts would be paid for by cheque, and if we should have occasion and opportunity to purchase fresh horses our cheques, endorsed by Mr. Fetherston, would be readily accepted.

Mr. Berry, with the horses and waggons, left Adelaide within a week of our arrival there. Mr. Fetherston, Jack, and I, remained a week or ten days longer. It was arranged that we should join them at Port Augusta, whence the real start would be made. Most of the time thus gained Jack and I spent in trying to make ourselves as well acquainted as possible with the route we were to travel by, and its position with reference to the other parts of Australia. In the Government office there were several charts and plans which we were permitted to study and to copy. The route was in the main identical with Stuart's track, but of much of the northern extremity it seemed to us doubtful if it had ever been surveyed at all. Of the other parts, however, a good deal was known, and the creeks and ranges were laid down with much apparent precision. Parts of the route might prove to be almost impracticable after a dry season, but as far as our information went, the worst country would be met with, not in the far interior but somewhere between Port Augusta and a point a little north of Lake Eyre.

Mr. Fetherston, Jack, and I, left Port Adelaide for Port Augusta the first week in November in a slow little steamer that took near a week on the passage; and we had to stay nearly another week at Port Augusta before the overland party arrived. I remember nothing of Port Augusta except a very miserable public-house, at which we lodged, and the sand hills, long, low, and white.

On the th of November we were well on the road, and we hoped to reach Daly Waters in about three months, and Mr. Fetherston expected that the line would be open to Port Darwin in about three months more. I may as well say here that it was in fact opened in the month of August, just nine months after we left Port Augusta.

We travelled over a very miserable country for some weeks. Not a really green thing was to be seen, and water was very scarce and bad. And the heat was excessive, far worse than we found it on any other part of the route; far worse, indeed, than any heat that I have ever endured either in Australia or elsewhere.

But after we had passed Lake Eyre a little way the country and the climate began to improve. And we had pleasant enough travelling until we got far beyond Alice's Springs. We had reached or passed the seventeenth degree of latitude before the water began to get very scarce or the ground very difficult again. There was not much variety in the scenery. We passed through long tracts of wooded country, and again over nearly treeless plains, and again over a succession of low hills, some bald and some covered with forest. Though none of them attained any considerable height, they sometimes assumed very remarkable forms. We met several creeks whose course was in the main dry, with here and there, however, ponds or water holes from ten or twenty to several hundred feet long. At the larger ponds we often got a variety of water fowl, but in general along the route there was a great scarcity of game.

Mr. Berry had in his own special service a certain Australian black with whom Jack and I formed an intimate acquaintance—of which and of whom I must tell you something; for if it had not been for him Jack and I would never have left the beaten track, and so this book would never have been written.

His name was Gioro; that was the way we came to spell it,

18

although J o r o would perhaps have been the better and simpler spelling. He was the most remarkable Australian black that I have ever met, and I have met a great many under a great variety of conditions and circumstances, and I find myself unable to differ seriously from the common estimate which places them near the very end of the scale. As a general rule (and I have only known the one exception), they have no really great qualities, none of those which are sometimes attributed to other barbarous races, as, for instance, to the American red man and even to the negro. But Gioro had qualities that would have done honour to the highest race on earth. He always spoke the truth, and he seemed to take it for granted that those to whom he spoke would also speak the truth. He had lived with white men in the North, and they must have been fine fellows, for he spoke of them always with respect, whereas he spoke with disgust and contempt of certain mean whites of Adelaide who had attempted to cheat him in some way. He never put himself forward, but if he were put forward by others who were in power he accepted the position as his right quite simply. He was as honest as the sun, and he was loyal through and through. He had even the manner of a gentleman. Mr. Fetherston's tent was notably the largest in our camp, and the union jack floated over it on Sundays. And every Sunday all the officers and volunteers, that is to say, Mr. Fetherston, Mr. Berry and his assistant, Jack and myself, dined there in a sort of state; and it was Mr. Fetherston's wont to have in one of the men to make the number even. And Gioro took his turn with us two or three times and was far the best conducted of those who were so invited. His ease of manner was perfect: he was as gentle and suave as an English nobleman; there was not a spark of self-assertion about him, and yet there was, or there seemed to be, a quiet consciousness of equality with his entertainers. He was also very courteous without being in the least bit cringing. He was glad always to teach us anything that we didn't know and that he knew, and he was grateful for being taught something in turn. Jack, for instance, took a great interest in the boomerang, and Gioro took much pains to teach him how to use it and how to make it. Jack had been distinguished at Oxford for his athletics. And these were a great bond between him and Gioro. He taught him several athletic feats, and Gioro's great suppleness of body enabled him to acquire them readily.

It was curious to notice the impression which his character made upon the men. His name suggested a very ready abbreviation, and indeed, he was often known in the camp as "Jo." But I never heard any one but Jack address him so. And Jack, as I have said,

19

was more intimate with him than any of us. One day, quite near the beginning of the expedition, Mr. Fetherston called him "Sir Gioro." I don't quite know what he meant, probably nothing more than a humorous recognition of the black man's unassuming dignity. Anyhow, the title stuck, and one heard his name afterwards, quite as often with the addition as without it.

He had not been at all corrupted by his intercourse with white men. That intercourse had indeed been very limited. He had spent the greater part of two years with some settlers near the Gulf, and he learned there a sort of pigeon English which enabled him to converse with us. He had come to Adelaide with some of the party who had been engaged in one of the unsuccessful attempts to complete the northern extremity of the overland wire. His engagement with Mr. Berry was terminable at pleasure on either side. From the account which he gave of himself I should think that he was about twenty-five years old: he had visited his own people since the commencement of his sojourn with white men, and he intended to visit them again. I had learned all this from him before we were half-way to the Daly Waters.

One evening, after we had passed the tropic, we camped earlier than usual because we had come upon a creek where there were tracks of wallaby and other game, and Gioro was very busy setting snares for them and showing us how to make and set such snares. The occupation seemed to remind him of his sojourn with the white men near the Gulf. So when we sat down to smoke, Gioro, Jack and I, Gioro said, "Way there," pointing to the north-east after looking at the stars, "two three white men, sheep, two three, two three, two three, great many; one man not white man, not black man, pigtail man, and Gioro." "And what," said Jack, "were they doing there, and what were you doing there?" "Pigtail man cook, wash clothes, white man ride after sheep, dogs too, Gioro ride, speak English, snare wallaby."

"How long did he stay there?" One year six months.

"How long since he left?" One year.

I will not give you much of Gioro's dialect; it was many days before I could readily understand him, and it was not a sort of dialect which is worth studying for its own sake. I learned from him that he belonged to a strong and populous tribe which occupied part of the country to the west of the Daly Waters. They had a king or chief whom Gioro held in the highest regard. His name was Bomero: the accent on the first syllable and the final "o" short like the "o" in rock. This Bomero was a great warrior and a mighty strong man, and possessed of great personal influence. It was my

20

fate, as you shall hear, to make his acquaintance, and I found him by no means the equal of Gioro in any of the greatest qualities of the man or the gentleman. Like some public leaders among more civilised people he owed his position partly to his fluent persuasiveness, partly to his violent self-assertiveness, and more than all to what I must call his roguery. Black men and white men are wonderfully like in some things.

Bomero seemed to have attained his power on the strength of these endowments alone. At least I could not learn anything decisive about his ancestry. Indeed, I could not gather that his people had any but the most elementary sense of the family relation, although tribal feeling, as distinct from family feeling, was very strong among them. Gioro had some recollection of "Old man Bomero," and his recollections would sometimes appear to indicate that Old man Bomero was a remarkable black fellow, but I could not discover that he ever attained to any position of special eminence among them. He certainly had not been their king as Bomero was.

I was at this time beginning to have some thought of a couple of days' expedition into the unexplored country to the west of the Daly Waters, and I had hinted as much to Jack. And I thought that the present was a good opportunity to find how far Gioro might be depended on as a guide. So I filled his pipe with my own tobacco (he was quite able to distinguish and prefer the flavour), and then I gave Jack a look to bespeak his attention, and began to put my questions.

"When would Sir Gioro see his own people again?"

Several slow puffs, a keen, eager, honest look, yet, withal, a cautious look, and then,

"May be one two months."

Then I said, "No water out west—die of thirst?"

"Now," said Gioro, nodding his head affirmatively, "but in one two months, no, no."

I saw that he meant either that after three months there would be wet weather, or that within three months we should have a better-watered country westward. So I said, pointing west, "What's out there?"

"No water, no grass, no duck, no black fellow."

"But," said I, looking northward, "we go on one two months, and then?" making a half-turn to face the west.

"Then," said he, "plenty grass, plenty fish, plenty duck, plenty black fellow."

"Everywhere?" said I, sweeping my arm all round the horizon.

"No, no, here, there, there. Gioro know the way, Bomero know the way, find Bomero, find water."

21

"What," said I, not understanding him, "Bomero make rain?"

But he replied with great contempt, "Bomero make rain! No, no. Bomero not witchfellow. No fear. Bomero make witchfellow make rain."

I think it was on this occasion that we ascertained that Gioro fully intended to go away westward in search of his tribe, who, as he expected, would be found in about three months at a point with which he was familiar at some uncertain distance from the Daly Waters.

They kept a great feast every year. It seemed to have some connection with the Pleiades and Aldebaran, for it was always celebrated when these stars were in conjunction with the sun. Several kindred tribes kept it, each in his own place westward, and every three years all the tribes who kept the feast celebrated it all together in a place farther west still. The triennial celebration was approaching, and Gioro intended to be there. He knew the way by which Bomero and his people would be travelling; he would cross their course, meet them, and go with them to the trysting-place.

Jack suggested that he and I and Gioro should all go together and visit his tribe.

Gioro hesitated for a little while, but after some apparently careful thought he said yes, he thought we could go.

After that we often talked it over with him, learning from him what we could about the disposition of his tribesmen towards white men, and about the distance of the triennial meeting-place of the tribes. It was quite impossible to say how far or how near this meeting-place might be; and on this depended in my judgment the practicability of the scheme. But at least, I thought, if the black fellows were friendly we might, under Gioro's guidance and protection, see a good deal of strange life and return home in a few days by the way we came. As far as I could gather, Gioro was the only one of his tribe that had ever seen a white man, although they had often heard of them, and curiosity rather than fear seemed to have been for some time the dominant feeling about them. But quite lately, for some reason or other, their fear began to exceed their curiosity.

The cause of this change was evidently something that had happened in the far west; some encounter with white men as Jack and I thought at first. But we had reason afterwards, as you will hear, to think that we were mistaken.

One evening I said to Gioro, "When did you see your people last?" He looked at the stars, and I knew he was going to be exact. Then he said, "One year."

"Did you tell Bomero then about the white men?"

"Yes, tell Bomero. Bomero never see white man."

"What did Bomero say?"

"Bomero say, white man all same dibble dibble."

"But Bomero never saw dibble dibble?"

"Yes, Bomero saw dibble dibble one, two, three, two two, two three, great many."

"Where?"

"Far away west."

"Where black fellows meet every three years?"

"More far."

"Bomero saw white men, not dibble dibble."

"No fear, Bomero saw dibble dibble and run away. Bomero run away from no man, black man, pigtail man, white man; but Bomero run from dibble dibble."

"Did any black fellow but Bomero see dibble dibble?"

"Yes, two three black fellow, more, all run away."

"And what like was dibble dibble?"

"White man all same dibble dibble."

That was all I could ever get out of him on the subject.

I spoke to Mr. Fetherston about our purpose of going westward with Gioro. He shook his head very gravely. "Well, Easterley," said he, "if you will be guided by me you will do nothing of the sort. You see we know next to nothing of those north-west blacks, and if you go it is even betting that you never come back. If you get, say, a hundred miles west of here you will be entirely dependent on the blacks. You will have to live among them, and to live as they live, if they let you live at all."

"But we have our compasses and the telegraph line."

"That would be all very well if it were a country through which you could make a 'bee line.' But you will want water and food, and you cannot get either without the help of the blacks."

"But," said I, "Gioro will come back with us."

"Gioro is a very good fellow, but if I were you I would not put myself altogether in his hands like that. He won't understand your anxiety to get away; he will think you are very well as you are. His interest in his own people will make him careless about you."

"But I know Gioro well, and I should trust him anywhere." So said I, and Jack eagerly agreed with me.

"But," said Mr. Fetherston, "Gioro may die or may be killed; they fight a great deal, and those who have been among white men are often subject to special enmity."

23

"I expect we shall have to chance that," said Jack. "Any of us may die or be killed."

"Well, gentlemen, wilful men you know—— I don't pretend to any right to constrain you, only let it be fully understood that if you go, you go against my wish and in defiance of my advice."

We agreed that everyone should know that, and so the matter dropped.

The road was now growing very difficult, the water scarcer, and the timber very much denser. But we pushed on little by little from day to day. We were ascending slowly the watershed between the north and south, and we had left behind us the last point to which the wire had yet been carried, when one morning Mr. Fetherston, after a specially careful observation, announced that within three days we might expect to meet the superintendent's party from the north, if all had gone well with them. The same afternoon Gioro took me aside, and told me that he meant to start the day after the next in search of Bomero and his people. We had come, he said, to certain landmarks that he recognised. The tribe would be already on the march, and he was confident that he could pick them up by following the water until it crossed their track. Next day was not Sunday, but we made a Sunday of it. We camped early, the Union Jack was hoisted, and Mr. Fetherston, the officers and volunteers, with one guest selected from the men in charge of the teams, sat down to dinner together. The man selected was a bushman of great and well-known experience, and, like Mr. Fetherston, he had been with Stuart on one or more of his exploring expeditions. I guessed from his presence that Mr. Fetherston intended that I should before the evening was over state my intention of going westward. Accordingly, when dinner was over and as we were about to light our pipes, I said before them all,

"Well, Mr. Fetherston, my friend Wilbraham and I are going to leave you for a few days at least. We propose to go westward with Sir Gioro, in order to see something of the aborigines. We may be back within a week, but we may push on with the blacks into the interior, and perhaps we may make for the north-west or west coast."

Mr. Fetherston turned to the man of whom I spoke just now and said:

"Well, Tim, what do you say to that?"

The man turned to me and said: "I didn't quite catch all you said, governor. Would you mind saying it again?"

I repeated what I had said. "Well," he replied, "it has been a main wet season out north, that I can see, and if you don't go more

24

than forty or fifty miles from the track you may get back within a week safe enough." He paused for a moment, and looked me steadily in the face, and went on—

"But, governor, if you go for the second part of the programme you'll never see a white man again."

"Why so?" said I.

"Well," said he, "you are depending on Gioro. Now Gioro is a good fellow, far the best black fellow I ever knew by a very long way. And my best hope for you is that Gioro will take you back once he has had a look at his people. He will, if he knows what will happen as well as I know it."

"And what will happen?" said I.

"Well, they'll kill Gioro before he has been very long among them. Sooner or later they always kill the blacks that have been among white men."

"And then," struck in Jack, "I suppose they will kill us."

"They may and they may not. You have ten times a better chance that Gioro. But if they don't you will be as good as their slaves for life. You won't be able to get back unless they take you back, and they will never take you back."

"Suppose we start to return on our own account?"

"Well," said the man, "if you are not more than forty or fifty miles to the west of the wire when you make the start eastward, and if you are able to make straight for the wire you may get back. But if you are much further away, or if you have to go a long way round you'll die of thirst or hunger in the bush." I noticed that he put thirst first.

"And, mind," he went on, "the chances are that you will be three times fifty miles to the west before you think of turning back."

"Why?"

"Because it's easy enough to travel with the blacks, easy enough for men of your sort, men that are hardy and are up to larks. The blacks know how to get food and water and fire, and you can live while in their company. It's only when you leave them that you will be done for."

Here Jack chimed in again. "Never mind," said he, "Mr. Easterley and I are going to try it, win or lose. Besides, after what you have told us, I wouldn't let poor 'Jo' go alone. We'll save him and he'll help us."

The answer came slowly. "Jo is your trump card, certainly ... and your only one."

Then Fetherston spoke. "Gentlemen, if I were your master I should absolutely forbid you to go, but I have not the right to interfere with your liberty. But I am glad that you have had the benefit of Mr. Blundell's experience." (Mr. Blundell was Tim.) "His opinion and mine coincide exactly."

"Well," said I, "Mr. Fetherston, we will be careful and we will bear in mind your advice, and I think it is on the whole most probable that you will see us back within the week."

"Possible," said Jack.

They all looked very sober then, and nothing more was said on the subject, and indeed little on any subject until the company broke up.

CHAPTER V

AMONG THE BLACKS

Our preparation for this madcap expedition was very soon made. We took our horses, for on foot we could not keep up with Gioro, and it was better to have the full benefit of his fleetness. We strapped our blankets to the pommels of our saddles. Jack carried a small fowling-piece, and I carried a pistol. We both had serviceable knives. A few small packages of tea and tobacco and what we thought a fair supply of ammunition completed our impedimenta.

We left our spare horse in charge of our man, and entrusted Mr. Fetherston with a cheque sufficient to pay the man's wages and to give him a small gratuity on his return to Adelaide. Meantime he was to be in Mr. Fetherston's service until we should rejoin the expedition, and if we did not rejoin it before its return to Adelaide then Tim Blundell was to have the horse. Early in the forenoon Gioro showed me a hill which seemed to be about ten miles away (it proved to be much further). He told us that at the foot of that hill we should find a creek which we had crossed at an earlier part of its course the afternoon before, and that creek we must follow down. Mr. Fetherston had the same hill marked on his chart, and his instructions were that when he was abreast of it he was to turn to the right nearly at right angles. So that when he should make this turn that must be our signal for parting with him. As we did not get abreast of the hill until it was rather late in the afternoon, we camped a little earlier than usual, and Gioro, Jack, and I deferred our departure until the next day. Shortly after sunrise we bade adieu to our friends with those noisy demonstrations on both sides which often serve the Englishman as a decent veil for those deeper feelings which he nearly always hesitates to show. The landscape here consisted of grassy slopes and plains, alternating with belts of well-forested country. We were in the middle of a plain when we parted from our fellow-travellers, and our courses were not in quite opposite directions; ours was about north-west, and theirs east-north-east. So while we remained in the plain we could see our fellow-travellers by simply looking to the right, and they us by looking to the left. So for a while there was much waving of hats on both sides. But the first belt of timber that we entered hid them from our sight. And then I think for the first time I became fully aware of the meaning of what we were doing.

"Jack, my boy!" said I, giving my horse a slight cut, so that he bounded forward, "we're in for it now."

"You don't seem sorry for it, Bob," said he, urging his horse to join me.

Truly neither of us was sorry for it. A new spirit of independence and love of adventure sprang up within us. We were young and well and strong. The morning air was fresh; the unaccustomed aspect of the forest, the screams of a flock of savage birds of the cockatoo sort that seemed as if they were making for the same hill as ourselves, the aspect of our native guide, who trotted on with his body slightly bent forward, and with the confident air of one who had "been there before," all stirred us to a sense of strangeness and expectance which was quite a joy. Even the warnings of Mr. Fetherston and Tim Blundell seemed only to intensify the joy.

"For if a path be dangerous known,
The danger's self is lure alone."

All the way from Port Augusta, Gioro had been dressed like the rest of us; he had worn a pair of moleskin trousers, a flannel shirt, and a cabbage-tree hat. But now he had discarded all these, and he wore nothing but a kilt of matting and a head-dress which consisted of a string bound round his brows adorned with the tails of the small wild animals of the bush and one large opossum tail hanging down behind. He ran on steadily towards the hill, which we reached in three or four hours from the start. It was rather a remarkable hill, as we saw when we reached it. Sloping gradually from the side on which we approached, it was on the opposite side steep and even precipitous. The creek ran on the far side, and the shadow of the hill lay still across it. It was about half-past ten when we reached it, and we rested until about an hour after noon. We made a can of tea and drank it. We had neither milk nor sugar, but we had a few biscuits and some slices of meat. Jack and I wondered where our next meal was to come from, but Gioro did not seem at all anxious. We could not, however, get a word out of him about the matter except "plenty duck."

We made a start in the direction of west by north, or thereabouts, Gioro leading the way and we following blindly. He ran more carefully and rather more slowly, but there was still the same air of confidence about him. It was now very hot, but as we were

28

well within the tropics, and the sun at noon was now as nearly as we could reckon vertical, the only wonder was that it was not much hotter. We must have been still high up on the watershed, although descending it on the northern slope. There was plenty of grass everywhere, and a good deal of timber, not so much, however, as to obstruct our passage or impede our view. The country was undulating, but there were no steep hills to be traversed. We passed a considerable herd of kangaroo and two or three dingoes, and there were many birds, chiefly crows, parrots, and cockatoos.

It was getting near sundown when we reached the summit of one of those low hills, and Gioro clapped his hands and shouted. We saw nothing but another hill, but it was clear that he recognised it, for he clapped his hands again and again, pointed towards it and said, "Plenty duck." He did not shape his course so as to cross the hill, but made for the point where it merged into the plain. And when we reached that point a sudden turn revealed a beautiful sheet of water, not very wide, but several hundred yards long, and consisting of two parts lying nearly at right angles to each other. This was the same creek which we had passed in the morning, but here it was much wider and deeper. Gioro stopped short and signed to us to stop. We did so at once, for we saw that the farther part of the water was alive with duck, and on the wider part nearer to us were several black swans. We turned immediately towards a grove of trees that lay between us and the water, and we dropped down. Gioro laid his hand on me, looked at Jack, pointed to the water and said, "Shoot." Jack stole to the water-side and shot a swan easily. It was not very near the others and none of the birds flew away. It was most likely the first time that firearms had been discharged there. Jack then shot several ducks and rejoined us. Gioro threw off his kilt and swam out for the birds. The moment his woolly head was seen over water all the birds flew away. We lit a fire at once, prepared and cooked our birds, and made a hearty meal. As we began to eat I remembered for the first time that we had no salt. I suppose I made a wry face, for Gioro grinned and pointed to a small bag which was fastened outside his kilt. This was full of salt, which he had thoughtfully provided for the dainty appetites of his white friends.

We slept sound and long that night, and in the morning Jack and I had a delicious bath, and washed our shirts and dried them in the sun. Going back to our camp we found a pleasant surprise awaiting us. Gioro had snared some wild creature—I think it was a bandicoot—and had baked it for breakfast. It was very nice, at least we thought so, and he was quite delighted when he saw that we enjoyed it. After breakfast we made an early start.

Two more days passed like this one. Each evening Gioro guided us to water and food, and all the time our course was in the main west by north or west-north-west. It was clear that we were following some river or creek downward, and so there were considerable occasional variations in the direction that we took, but we never headed south of west or east of north. On the morning of the third day Gioro speared a large fish. I think it was a variety of perch; it was very good eating.

This third morning we left the creek nearly at right angles and struck across the forest, and our guide was evidently more sharply on the watch than ever. He travelled very slowly now and he seemed to be looking everywhere for some local indications. After about two miles travelling we came again upon a creek, as far as I could judge a different one. It was very narrow and scarcely running. There was one very fair pond, however, but Gioro took scarce any notice of it, but ran on to the dry or nearly dry bed of the creek beyond. Here he set up a triumphant yell, and signed to us to come and see. I saw plainly enough what I thought at first to be a cattle track coming from the north-east and passing right across the bed of the creek. I looked at Gioro and said, "Sheep?" "No, no," he shouted, "not sheep; black fellow, black fellow," and stooping down he pointed at the track. I stooped also and examined it, and sure enough I could see plainly the mark of human feet. "When shall we catch them up, Sir Gioro?" said I. "To-night," he shouted; "to-night, Corrobboree! Corrobboree!"

We followed the track without pause, and by-and-by more tracks joined it, all from the north or east or from some point between these. There could be no doubt at all that we were approaching some camping-place of the blacks. Our course was now almost directly westward, with a very slight trend to the north, and the country still continued much of the same sort, undulating perhaps a little more, well grassed and fairly but not very thickly timbered. Wild animals and birds were much more numerous.

It was after sunset, the moon which was now nearly half way between new and full was well up in the sky, there was a strange glimmer in the west that looked like an aurora, and Gioro was in a state of high excitement when the pathway bending round the foot of a somewhat steeper hill than we had seen during the day suddenly brought us within sight of a single fire. It was evidently just freshly kindled, but there was no one near it now. Gioro stopped, looked at us, and put his hand to his mouth. Then we made a half turn silently, still following the track, and all in a moment we came in view of the most striking sight that I had yet seen in Australia, or for the matter of that anywhere in the world.

We saw an irregular line of large fires burning before us, and immediately behind them stretched a sheet of water much wider and longer than any that we had yet seen in the country. The fires were vividly reflected in the water, and seemed at the first glance quite innumerable. After a time one saw that there were at least sixty or eighty of them. Near each fire was a group of black men, clad like Gioro, holding in their hands long staves or spears, and dancing furiously. They kept springing into the air with their feet quivering, and striking their spears, butt ends downwards, violently upon the ground. Presently they burst into a wild shout, or series of shouts. The shouts came in measured cadence, but were frightfully discordant. Their dance kept time to their music, and the whole effect was wildly barbarous. There were huts in great numbers built of branches, and covered with leaves and bark. As far as I could see there was a hut for each fire, and women and children of all ages were to be seen in front of the huts, some few of them apparently partaking of the excitement of the dancers, but far the greater number stolidly looking on. The dress of the women was nearly the same as that of the men. The kilt of matting was the same, but the head-dress showed more effort after ornament. It covered more of the head, and it was adorned with the feathers of cockatoos and parrots. The children who ran about were mostly naked. There were several dogs, not at all Australian dingoes, but miserable half-starved mongrels of European breed. Many of the women were engaged in cooking food, and some whiffs of smoke which reached us were by no means of unpleasant flavour.

All the while the song and dance lasted we lay quite still, hidden by the scrub which grew very thick here, and seemed to be a sort of stunted eucalyptus, and very like the mallee of Southern Australia. Our horses were hidden by the turn of a hill, and by a large tree near, and when the song and dance would pause for a moment, we could hear them munching the grass. I was at first greatly afraid that they would be startled by the noise and by the fires, but somehow they seemed to take no notice. They were accustomed to camp fires and singing, but not to such singing as that. When the song and the dance were ended, Gioro touched us, pointed and whispered, "Bomero, boss black fellow, see!" We looked in the direction of his finger, and could easily see a very tall and bulkily built black, with a very massive head, and dressed with some attempt at distinction. His kilt of matting was larger than any of those worn by the others, and was rather elaborately ornamented

31

with feathers. His head-dress was very much larger, and he wore besides a sort of little cloak of skins thrown over his shoulder, and fastened with some kind of thong. Gioro whispered again, "Stay! Gioro speak to Bomero, then come back." With this he stood erect, spear in hand, and advanced towards the fire where the tall black stood, dancing all the time rather gently, and singing rather softly, but exactly the same step and tune which we had just heard and seen. We followed him closely with our eyes, and we were in a state of great excitement and suspense.

He was noticed almost immediately, but there was hardly any sign of surprise, and none at all of hostility. I suppose that his dance and song secured him for the time from either. Bomero stepped out to meet him, followed by three or four other blacks. Gioro continued his dance and song till he came quite up to them, and then he went round them still dancing and singing. He stopped right in front of Bomero. And there seemed to follow a sort of obeisance and salutation, and then a palaver.

As the palaver proceeded the blacks became greatly excited, and more of them gathered round. No doubt he was telling them about us. I felt for my pistol, and looked towards the horses. I could still hear them munching the grass.

Presently Gioro came towards us, looking quite cheerful and confident. He told us that Bomero wished to see us and bid us welcome. We fetched our horses, and we led them with us, holding ourselves in readiness to mount at a moment's notice.

As we marched up to the camp great excitement prevailed, and we were presently surrounded by a vast concourse of men, women, and children. Some half dozen of the blacks around Bomero armed themselves with boughs of trees, and kept the crowd at a sufficient distance.

Bomero came towards us with spear in hand, and two men on each side of him also with spears. We made a sort of military salute, which he seemed to understand, and made an attempt to return. Then he began to talk. When he ceased, I turned to Gioro and said, "What says Bomero?"

Gioro looked first at Bomero, and then at me, then quite rapidly, "Bomero, say, know all about white fellow; white fellow ride on horse, keep cattle, keep sheep, carry fire spear. Bomero say white fellow hold fire spear in hand, throw away only point, but point kill. Sometime one point, sometime two, three points, two three. Bomero say, Good-morrow to white fellow. White fellow all same black fellow. Black fellow take white fellow to great Corrobboree far

32

away west when the one[2] white star rise, and red star and little stars go."

I replied with all the dignity that I could muster, "Right, all right; say to Bomero, 'thanks.' King Bob and king Jack all same king Bomero. King Bob and king Jack will go with king Bomero to great Corrobboree when the one white star rises, and the red star and the little stars go."

Then we were told that our miami must be built and that we must have meat and sleep, as we should have to start with the sun. They fell to work, Gioro and two or three others, and built a sort of hut in an incredibly short time, and then we supped on fish and wild duck and paste made with water of the seeds of some native grass. I think it was "nardoo." We had also a fruit which I have seen nowhere else, about the size of a loquat, of a pinkish colour and subacid in taste. After supper we had a palaver, Gioro being the interpreter, and then we went to bed. Jack and I slept well and rose before sunrise in order to get a bath before starting. Several of the blacks followed us to the water's edge and some of them plunged into the water after us. I didn't half like it as they swam round and round us; but they were more afraid of us than we of them.

Then we breakfasted and made a start. For twelve days we travelled on, still heading mainly westward, running down a watercourse, then crossing to another. Bomero was the leader always, and he seemed to know the way quite well. We always camped at water, and when we crossed from one creek to another the distance was usually no more than three or four miles. We passed a good many hills, but none of them I should say rising more than a thousand feet from the plain, and few of them so much as that. As far as I could reckon we must have travelled twenty-five to

---

[2] The red star is certainly Aldebaran, and the little stars the Pleiades. I could not for a long time understand "the one white star." There is at present no large white star in opposition to Aldebaran. I first thought that Arcturus might be meant, and that the feast had perhaps come down from a period when Arcturus was a white star. But I now think that Spica Virginis is "the one white star." I think that by "rises," or more properly, "has risen," Gioro meant "has culminated;" for Gioro usually spoke of "rising" and "setting" as "coming" and "going;" so if he had meant to speak of stars in opposition he would have said, "when the white star comes and the red star goes." Spica culminates about the time that Aldebaran sets; also there are no large stars near Spica, and this may be why it is called "the one white star." I think I have read that some people for the same reason call it "the lonely one." Gioro probably meant, "When the lone white star has culminated, and the red star and the little stars are set."—R. E.

thirty miles a day, and the greater part of that was westing. I believe that on the evening of the twelfth day after we fell in with Bomero's people we must have been all of three hundred or three hundred and fifty miles to the west of the telegraph wire.

During those twelve days we did our best to study the people and the country so as to prepare ourselves for anything that might happen. Jack made a rough chart of each day's march, and we both made an attempt to keep a sort of dead reckoning. It was very hard, however, to make any available record of our observations. The curiosity and perhaps the suspicion of the blacks made it next to impossible to write or draw by daylight, and at night we had only the light of our fires and a sort of torch that we managed to make of bark and fat.

We were beginning to know something of the language. There was a palaver every night, or, to speak more exactly, there were several palavers, in one of which we always joined, with Gioro for interpreter. And on several occasions Bomero harangued the tribe. These harangues were very interesting, even before we could understand any part of them or before Gioro explained a word of them. The manner and mode of delivery were very remarkable. Bomero was highly demonstrative, but he was never carried away by his own eloquence. The spirit of the prophet was always subject to the prophet. He could pull himself together in a moment and be as cool as you please. The matter of his harangues was chiefly the greatness of his tribe, and above all of the king of the tribe, the king's ability to guide his people to food and water, to beat any two or three men of his own tribe, and as many as you like of any other tribe, the great Corrobboree that they were going to keep out away west, and the greatness of the tribes who kept it, of which tribes they were the greatest, and Bomero was the greatest of them.

These harangues were his method, it seemed, of keeping up his influence over his people in time of peace. And one could not but liken him, as Carlyle says, to "certain completed professors of parliamentary eloquence" nearer home.

The Pleiades were now seen to be setting earlier and earlier every evening. They were for a few nights obscured by clouds, and the next time they appeared they were perceptibly nearer the sun. This fact was observed at once and they hailed it with what at first seemed to be a series of shouts, but which proved to be a sort of barbaric chant, each stave of which ended with this refrain:—

"Go, go,
Red star and little stars."

34

And this was a chant as Gioro told us (and Bomero confirmed him) which their fathers and their fathers' fathers had sung before them from time immemorial. I wish that some of our savants would investigate this matter, for I cannot but think that this festival and its obvious connection with the constellation Taurus would throw some important light on the origin of these people and their connection with the other races of mankind.

Jack and I for obvious reasons gave them some illustrations of the use of our "fire spears." Mine they said was a "fire spear" of one point, and Jack's of two three points, two three; that is to say I used a bullet and Jack used shot. We were beginning to be favourites, and even Bomero himself liked us, for although he showed at first some signs of being jealous, we treated him with such deference that he soon forgot his jealousy. Jack had a black leather belt for wearing round the waist, and we made Bomero a formal present of this. We explained its use to him and put it round his kilt. We could see that he was nearly overcome with childish delight, and yet the wily fellow was knowing enough to repress all show of this feeling and to receive the gift with stolid gravity. He gave us in turn an eagle's feather each, which he took off the kilt just where the belt would cover it, and these we received with becoming gratitude.

A serious misfortune befell us about the eighth day, which was the occasion of another compliment to Bomero. Jack's horse fell dead lame, and we were obliged to let him loose in the bush. We presented the saddle to our black prince, and made a throne of it for him, and one evening that we camped earlier than usual we persuaded him to hold a levee. Jack explained the matter to Gioro, and Gioro to Bomero. This was how Jack explained it.

Gioro. What's levee?

Jack. Boss white fellow stands on daïs. No, sits on throne, throne all same saddle and stirrups; other white fellows march up, march down again, come this way, go that way, all same little stars and red star. Bow to boss white fellow. Boss white fellow bows to them. Boss black fellow all same boss white fellow.

Bomero took readily to the proposal. We picked out a fallen tree high enough and wide enough. We fixed up the saddle upon it, the stirrups touching the ground. Bomero got astride of this with a spear in each hand. I passed before him bowing, and Jack followed me. All the others followed him. They took to it as if they had been born courtiers. They would not be satisfied until every adult man had made his bow, and we had something to do to keep them from beginning all over again. It was ludicrous to the last degree. The tall, bulky black fellow sat on the saddle with the tree under him like a

35

hobby-horse, his head was all stuck over with feathers and the tails of opossums; his little cloak of skins and kilt of platted leaves were fastened with Jack's belt, and he held his two spears, one in each hand, and he looked as sober and solemn as a judge, and the other fellows as much in earnest as if they were freemasons in full regalia, or doctors of divinity in academic dress. I stole a look at Jack, and the villain replied with one of those winks which never fail to upset me. He let the lid of one eye fall completely, the other eye remaining wide open, and not a wrinkle in his face. A loud laugh would have spoiled the fun, and might even have been dangerous, but I saved myself with a fit of coughing. After the levee Bomero told off two men to have charge of the saddle. And for the next few days Jack and I walked, each of us, half the march, and rode the other. Once only during these twelve days did I see anything to give me any special uneasiness. One evening we camped a little earlier than usual and I noticed that Gioro was watched and dogged by two very ill-looking fellows whom I had noticed as being in some sort leaders. They stepped behind a clump of trees as he was passing, and as he returned they hid themselves again while he passed. I mentioned this to Gioro and he proved to be aware of their hostility. They were big men, he said, in the tribe, but Bomero was the biggest of all the men, and he was Gioro's friend.

About the morning of the twelfth day there was some trouble. We had come to a point where it was necessary to leave the course of one creek and to strike that of another. But a very destructive fire had passed over the place, followed, as it seemed, by heavy rains, and the track was quite obliterated. Certain trees also which would have served as guides had been entirely destroyed. And to increase the confusion the weather was foggy. Dense clouds rested on and hid some hills which might have served as landmarks.

Bomero went out to reconnoitre, and he took Gioro and another with him, and when they returned I could see that his mind was made up as to the course he would take, but that he was, nevertheless, as much perplexed as ever. He gave the word and we struck out a little north of west, and after travelling about three times as far as it had yet taken us to get from water to water we struck another creek. We marched along the creek for another day, scarce ever losing sight of it, and then we camped by the water again. Next morning we left the women and children in camp, and about half the men, and Bomero with the ablest and quickest of the men marched away in search of another creek. Jack and I went with him, and as my horse was in good working condition we took him with us. We struck water somewhat sooner than before and camped for the night. I saw that Bomero was still perplexed, and I gathered from Gioro that his perplexity was caused by the conviction that he was now considerably out of his course, that he had gone too far north and had overshot the mark, and that we should have to go a day's march south and east before we could resume the straight course to the place of meeting. The horizon was still clouded, and there was no sign at present of the clouds lifting soon.

All this, however, was by no means enough to account for Bomero's evident perturbation of mind. He was undoubtedly a clever and cool fellow, and one of much resource; there was abundance of water and food, we could not be far out of the track, and we had plenty of time, for as far as I could judge by the astronomical indications, we were a great many days and even weeks too soon; and the weather, barring the clouds, was everything that could be wished.

Jack and I talked it over, and Jack reminded me of Gioro's tale of the "dibble dibble all same white man" that Bomero had seen in the far west. "Depend upon it," said Jack, "he thinks he is coming upon them again. The place, as Gioro said, was 'more far' than the place of meeting for the great Corrobboree, and he thinks that he is now getting 'more far' than there."

"And what of the dibble dibble that he saw there?" said I.

"Oh, that's the point," said Jack. "No doubt they were white men; some pioneers from the north coast, perhaps, or maybe the men on some outlying station of some western squatter's run, and if so we shall get back to civilisation sooner than we think."

"I don't see much in it, Jack," said I; "we're not far enough west for that; if we were on the head-waters of the western slope we might be on the look-out for white pioneers, but I am afraid we are near as far from there as from the telegraph wire. Bomero's 'dibble dibble' was either a pure invention or the suggestion of a dream, or if he did come across white men he must have been farther west than he is here."

On the morning of the fourteenth day Bomero harangued the men who were with him; he stood upon a veritable stump, a huge tree near the creek had been undermined by the flood waters and had fallen and lay along the ground roots and all. Bomero stood upon it and spoke, Jack and I stood by and listened, Gioro stood between us; he was in a state of great excitement, and he threw in every now and then a word of interpretation for our benefit, but indeed, by this time, we were able to follow the speaker fairly enough ourselves. It very soon became quite evident that Gioro's tale of "dibble dibble" was at the bottom of our trouble; it was quite

37

evident also that the spirit of the prophet was no longer subject to the prophet. Bomero pointed westward, where the clouds were now slowly rising from some not very distant hills, and what he said was to this effect.

There was a hill away west where certain doleful creatures dwelt. He had once been very near there, and they had tried to take his life. They had tried to spear him through the air, and he who never feared men, feared them. He should know in a few minutes if that hill yonder was their hill; and if it was then he and his people must run and run till they got well out of sight of that hill. They had missed the way to the great Corrobboree, but that was no matter; they would easily find it again, and there was plenty of time yet before the red star and the little stars would be gone. If they saw when the clouds rose (and they were now rising) that the hill was not their hill, then they would stay where they were to-day, and the witch fellows would dance the witch dance until all was clear, and on the next day they would go back to where the women were, and then they would strike the track, and be the first at the meeting-place. But if when the clouds rose, and they were now rising, they saw three peaks, a tall one in the middle, a crooked one on one side, and a straight one on the other, then Bomero and Bomero's men must run, run, run, and never stop, except to breathe, while any one of the three peaks was to be seen. Let the black man knock his brains out with his waddy, or let the white man spear him with his fire spear, but the devils that rode through the air on clouds, faster than eagles, were worse than any black men or white men.

Bomero was evidently no longer master of himself or of his men. Whatever the cause of it was, there was a dreadful panic imminent, and no one could tell what was going to happen.

Just then the clouds lifted quite away from the hill, and there, sure enough, were the three peaks, the tall one in the middle, and the crooked one and the straight one on either side.

A low murmur burst from the men, and Bomero uttered a frightful howl, and plunged away madly round a hill that rose gently from the creek, and right on into the forest. All the men ran after him, most of them howling and shrieking; and my horse, which hung by the bridle to a branch close by, started, and snorted, and broke his rein, and rushed away before them at full gallop.

The catastrophe was so sudden that our breath seemed to be taken away, and I don't know how many minutes passed before either spoke. I know that every man of the blacks had got clean out of sight, and my horse, too, and there was as dead a silence as before the world was made, and still there was not a word from either of us. Then Jack said in a hollow voice:

38

"Why wasn't the horse hobbled, Bob?"

"Why, Jack, I had just taken the hobbles off, and made him ready for the road."

"Never mind, old fellow, I hardly know what I said; Gioro will come back."

"Yes," I said, "Gioro will come back."

And then, as if our confidence in Gioro's fidelity cleared the air, we sat down and lit our pipes.

I don't know how much time passed, it seemed to be hours, but it couldn't have been near an hour, and Jack and I never exchanged a word. Then, sure enough, we saw Gioro coming, and he was leading my horse. I saw him first, and I jumped up and shouted for joy. Then Jack jumped up, but the shout died on his lips, and he said only, "There is something the matter."

And so there was. Both Gioro and the horse were wounded, and the wounds were deadly, for the spears that inflicted them were poisoned. The horse died first. I took Gioro's head on my lap, and gave him a few drops of water. He told me that he had caught the horse by the bridle in passing, and that then he stopped and returned. He had not forgotten us, he said, not for a moment, nor would he have started at all if the horse had not started. The horse had stopped several times, and when he had come up with him had gone on again. But at last he had secured him and was returning. But several spears were flung at him, and many missed him, but the big men who had watched and dogged him took better aim, and struck both horse and man. At first he thought nothing of it, but presently he knew that the spears were poisoned, and now he must die.

"Take care," said the poor fellow, almost with his last breath, "keep away, kill you too, like Gioro; back, back to the big long wire."

He died quite easily, and I felt as he lay in my arms that it would be the best thing that could happen us if the poisoned arrows of the blacks had made an end of us as well as of him. The poor fellow's faithfulness would have helped us to face death without flinching.

We found a large hole in the earth where a tree had been uprooted by a storm, and there, with the help of his boomerang and our own knives, we managed to give him decent burial. We both fell on our knees for a few minutes, but no words passed our lips, although I am sure our hearts were full enough.

Then we stood up, and with one impulse held out a hand each to the other. The grip that followed was a silent English grip. But it meant that we knew that our case was desperate, and that we would stand by one another to the last.

CHAPTER VI

LEFT ALONE

All the events described at the close of the last chapter succeeded one another very rapidly. I do not think that four hours in all could have passed from the beginning of Bomero's last harangue until Jack and I stood together over Gioro's grave. The sun had not reached the meridian; the atmosphere was perfectly clear; and the triple peak which had been the signal of so much disaster stood out clear and well-defined in the west.

What were we to do now? Were we to stay here and die like starved bandicoots when the first drought should come on? That was the question in both our minds, and that was the form in which Jack expressed it. "Let us get some food first," said I, "and then we shall see. Thank God it is easy enough still to get food." We soon lit a fire and shot some duck, and with the help of some of the wild fruit already mentioned and the water of the creek we did well enough. Then we talked over the situation, and it soon became clear that only two courses were open to us if we were to return to civilisation, or even to live. The one course was to push backward by the way we came. And if it had not been for the last two days' journey we should probably have chosen that way without hesitation. And even now if we could be sure of not meeting the blacks again, I think we might have tried it. It was true that we might wait here long enough to make sure that the blacks would have gone westward, but all the while we should wait, the tracks and the other waymarks would be gradually becoming obliterated. Besides, it was certain that we could not live by snaring birds and spearing fish for food as the blacks could, and our powder and shot would soon be done. Our better hope seemed to lie in the chance of finding white men somewhere near, and the strange proceedings of Bomero seemed surely to indicate the near presence of white men. He must have met some pioneers from the west coast. Such men were often known to treat the blacks as if they were mere wild beasts, and it seemed not unlikely that some act of reckless cruelty on the part of the white men might have been witnessed by him, or, at least, that he might have heard of such from some other blacks.

Jack had a little pocket telescope, and he examined the hill to westward with it. After a careful scrutiny he declared that he saw a man in one of the gaps on the top of the hill and that he was a white man. "Yes, I see him," said I, for I thought I observed something moving, "but I cannot say whether he is black or white." Jack handed me the glass, but I could not now distinguish even with the glass any sign of life or movement.

He took back the glass in a hurry and looked again, and then he declared that he could no longer see any man. "And yet," said he, "there was a man there, and he had on a long coat, and there was something odd and foreign in the look of him."

"Nonsense," I said, "you could never tell that at such a distance and with such a glass."

"Well, one would think not," he said, "and yet it was as I say."

I then went over my calculations with a view to determine whereabouts we were, but I could not by any means make our position far enough west to render it likely that we were near any settlement. We had no instrument by which we could make observations with any approach to accuracy. Our latitude was not much changed since we had left the wire; that much we could see from the stars. But our course had been so very zigzag that it was quite impossible to estimate our longitude within a hundred or more miles. And even if our course had been due west all through I still could hardly think that we were near the head waters of the western slope. After all, however, it seemed the wisest course to reconnoitre, first, this mountain or hill. If there was no one there it would be still possible for us to return to where we were now, and to make a start eastward. Indeed, if the hill were not inhabited, that would be the only course that would be in the least degree hopeful. For certainly to strike westward without any guide or any knowledge of the way would be for us, and in such a country as Australia, to face certain death.

We made up our minds, therefore, to explore the hill at once. We put together somehow the remains of our breakfast, enough for two very spare meals each. We took a good drink of water and filled with water a small flask which would suffice to moisten our lips and throats in case we should find none at the hill. We reckoned that the hill was not quite ten miles away, and if that were all, we should get there in time to reconnoitre while it was still daylight, and if no prospect of help appeared we would return early in the morning. Then we took our farewell of poor Gioro's grave and set our faces to the hill. The way was quite easy; there was but little timber and the grass, although thick, was short. There were still evidences about us that the past season had been wet, but we did not find the ground boggy, and the atmosphere was fresh, clear, and bright. As we marched forward the shape of the hill became better and better defined, and more striking. It stood quite alone in the plain, from which it seemed to rise sheer upward with little or no slope.

It looked for all the world as if it had been dropped from the sky, so completely without connection was it with the surrounding landscape. As we drew nearer, it presented more the appearance of a huge irregular building which had become covered in the course of ages with vegetation. But, as we drew nearer still, these odd appearances gradually wore away, and it began to look not very unlike other lonely and precipitous rocks which I have seen in Australia. Such a rock, for example, as the Hanging Rock, near Woodend, only very much larger, or such a rock as that other one a little north of the Billabong, and south of the Murrumbidgee, near the railway between Albury and Wagga.

As we drew near the foot of the precipice we made for the shadiest spot that we could find.

The various crags of which the hill was formed were covered almost everywhere with a foliage which differed but little from the prevailing Australian type.

There was abundance of the sweet smelling shrub which is common along the shores of Port Phillip. I pressed and rubbed a few of the leaves and the smell was just the same. There was less of the blue gum and more of the lightwood than I had elsewhere seen, and there were a good many pines. There were also a few remarkable shrubs that I have not seen elsewhere, and a few large and queer-looking flowers of a bright red colour.

We made for this particular spot not only because it was the shadiest but because it seemed to have a fresher and greener look than the rest of the hill; and our delight was great when upon reaching it, and after poking about a little while, we found a large basin or pond of water surrounded and shut off by rocks. It was nearly elliptical in shape but rather elongated: about thirty feet by ten. The water seemed at first as if it issued from the earth, but on closer inspection we had little doubt that it was due altogether to the rainfall percolating through the cliffs from the heights above.

Here we sat and refreshed ourselves for an hour or so before consulting as to our further progress.

It was later than we had reckoned on, for the journey to the hill had taken a longer time than we thought it would take; so we resolved to decide nothing further until the morning.

We chose not to light a fire although we knew by experience that the middle of the night would be very cold. We told ourselves that though we had seen no sign of any more natives there were probably some about, and therefore that it was better not to light a fire. Our prevailing reason, however, was an indefinite sense of dread which had come upon us and which we confessed to one another as we sat and ate.

We chose to attribute this dread to the strange and threatening shape of the hill as we approached it. Yet as we looked about us now we could not but acknowledge that we had seen many more awful cliffs and precipices without any of the unreasonable feeling which we could not but confess to now. A little while before sunset I noticed something which I tried to tell myself was most likely nothing, but which, nevertheless, increased this indefinite fear into a sense almost of horror.

The sky was perfectly cloudless, but for all that the shadow of a cloud fell on the ground quite near. The sun was very low and the shadows were nearly at their longest, and yet about this there was a shapeliness too definite for a cloud, a sort of shapeliness which might have reminded me at once of those other shadows of which I have told you, and yet it did not then remind me of them. It was the same sort of shadow, only elongated by the setting sun. It passed away very rapidly and I said nothing of it to my companion who was dozing.

Indeed, I felt the same unaccountable unwillingness to speak of it that I felt when I had seen the like of it before.

Next morning we awoke early, and found to our great delight a second well of water higher up the cliff. It was very much smaller—only a few feet across, but it was purer; and we determined if we remained long here to reserve it for drinking and to bathe in the larger one.

After we had bathed and had eaten the few scraps of food which remained to us, we began to reconnoitre, and we were both immediately struck by the appearance of the ground a few hundred yards to the south of where we had slept, but still at the foot of the cliff. The ground was worn away, it might be by water, it might be by some heavy mass being dragged along it.

It had a curious air of something like regularity, which suggested, and yet which need not suggest, art or design. We saw, however, at once, that it was the termination of a sort of hole in the cliff, apparently coming from above.

As this hole proved to be quite large enough for three or four men to stand up in it abreast, and as the ascent of it seemed not impracticable, we began to think of trying to ascend it.

Jack thought that it might lead us to the top more easily than the surface of the hill. Certainly no part of the cliff, as far as we had

43

seen, seemed at all practicable, but I saw no reason to suspect that we should find a readier passage upward here. Still I agreed with Jack that we might as well try it. I insisted, however, that only one of us should go up, and that the other should await either his return or some signal from the top, if that were possible.

We agreed finally to cast lots to see who should stay behind, and the lot fell upon Jack. I immediately began the ascent, and found it very much easier than I had expected. The darkness increased only for a little while, and by and by it began to grow light, and I then discovered a sort of roadway with steps moulded out of the soil on either side.

After perhaps an hour of this work I came suddenly to a level. The passage opened into a spacious cave, which was dimly lit by a large opening in the rock, across which there seemed to be growing a thick scrub, not so thick, however, but that here and there the sunshine came freely enough through.

I had little doubt now that I was coming upon some hiding place of the blacks, and I proceeded with very great caution. I made slowly for the opening in the rock of which I had spoken, and when I had nearly reached it I saw that I could, without very much difficulty, force my way through the scrub. On a closer approach I observed with great astonishment that the scrub seemed to be arranged in two square pieces, which were certainly suggestive of a gateway.

There was a framework of dead branches, or rather two frames, and the scrub was roughly twisted in and out upon these. I thought it best now to make some preliminary observation from behind the screen of leaves and branches.

I soon found a small opening where I could see without any risk of being seen. I looked cautiously through. What I saw I will tell you in the next chapter.

Note.—I have never been able to come to any decisive conclusion as to the origin and use of this cave or underground passage by which I made the ascent to the gateway as above described. It was in no way necessary, as far as I could see, to the people of whom you will read in the following chapters. I should have thought it an old haunt of the blacks but for two reasons: If it had been so it must have been long disused by them, and yet it was evidently still, or quite recently, in use, but for what purpose I am unable even to guess. I tell you the facts as I find them.—R. E.

CHAPTER VII

THE CARS

What I saw was this: a platform of rock extending before me a mile or nearly so, and about double the width of a very wide road. This platform ended in the cliff, which there bent suddenly into a line almost at right angles with the line of the platform. That was not straight but followed the slighter bends of the cliff. There were three flights of stone steps descending towards the valley, one of them at least, the broadest, reaching the whole way down. The valley itself seemed to be filled with houses and rows of trees, and certain enclosures that looked like gardens. The houses were odd-looking but unpretentious. One saw at a glance that their oddity was in the main owing to their lack of size, and to the absence of chimneys. One could not suppose them to be of much use for living in, and yet the whole appearance of the scene quite forbade one from accounting for their size by the poverty of the builders or from any other lack of resource.

But the scene closer at hand arrested my attention so forcibly that the more distant view left but a faint and general impression on my mind. On one side of the platform, the side next the valley, there were a number of men engaged at work of some sort, but their backs were just then turned to me: and I cannot tell you why, but the sight of men, probably civilised men, by no means gave me such hope or pleasure as our desolate condition would have justified.

On the other side of the platform, the side next the cliff, there were a number of objects which I must try to describe even at the risk of being tedious, as they proved to have a very decisive effect upon the progress and sequel of our adventures. They presented a most uncouth and bizarre appearance, and although they were all of one kind, almost identical in every detail, it was not until after several minutes' view of them that the fact of their likeness became apparent. Then I perceived that they were all some sort of conveyance consisting of an upper and lower framework. Here I saw a very odd-looking car resting on nothing at a distance of a few feet from the ground, and there I saw an elaborately constructed support which supported nothing. I saw, further, that the height of the supports was about as great as the distance of the cars from the ground, and I thought for a moment that by some unaccountable distortion of sight, the supports got the appearance of being separated from the things which were supported. But almost immediately I saw that this could not be the case, for in some instances it seemed as if the body of the car were cut into two parts, part only remaining and resting upon a complete frame; and then again, the body of the car was all there, and rested, for about half of its mass, on a supporting frame, half of which appeared to have been removed, while the other half of the body of the car appeared to be resting on nothing. A longer look at the scene offered an explanation, but it was an explanation which most urgently needed to be itself explained. At each of these objects a man stood, as it would seem, painting them, and he seemed to dip what I thought to be a brush in a bucket beside him. And at first I thought that he was painting the whole object, car and supporting framework, but presently I perceived that the brush which he was using and which showed a very irregular and jagged edge, never touched, or never at least was seen to touch anything at all, but that what it passed over disappeared. I watched the operation with breathless attention, and I saw the body of the car which had seemed to hang in the air gradually disappear as the brush passed over it, until nothing was left either above or below. I watched another which was complete in all parts until nearly the whole of the supporting framework disappeared beneath the brush. It looked for all the world as if some sort of invisible paint were being smeared over the conveyances. That they were conveyances of some sort I felt no doubt, but whether they were meant to travel on land or water I doubted. I saw no wheels, but these might be hidden by the framework, and there were things attached to each which might be said to have a remote resemblance to the screw of a steamboat. I may as well say at once that they proved to be carriages for travelling through the air.

Just then, some of the men who were working on the other side of the platform turned their faces towards me, and one of them, who seemed to be a sort of director or superintendent, came from behind them moving in the same direction. All kept moving towards where I stood until they were so near that I could clearly distinguish their features and their dress. The costume of all was exactly the same but unlike anything that I had ever seen. Each wore a low hat of a light colour and a broadish brim, a coat or smock reaching to the knee and fastened with a girdle, and some kind of shoe or sandal for the feet. That was all. As I noticed these points, the leader took a half-turn to the left and the men to the right, so that they and he stood facing one another with their side faces towards me. All the men were about as unlike one another as the same number of men

46

picked up anywhere at random, excepting for one point. They had all an expression of malignity which was horrible to look upon, and which was worse, if possible, in the side face than in the full face. Not that there was anything deformed about their countenances; quite the contrary. Every feature considered by itself, whether from the front or side-view, was remarkably well formed. Eyes, mouth, nose, teeth, and hair, were of just the size, shape, and colour that you would say they ought to be. In fact, the symmetry of their faces was ideally perfect, and attracted more notice than anything else in their appearance except one thing, and that one thing was the malignity of their expression. That was utterly inhuman; it was diabolical. I declare that as I stood there behind the forest scrub and watched them, my very heart sank. I felt that I would rather see a dozen man-eating tigers or a herd of hungry wolves. I am not constitutionally timid and yet I repressed with difficulty a cry of despair.

As I looked in sheer horror and terror I thought I caught sight among the faces of a face that I knew. But surely I had never seen anything so frightful in my waking moments. Could I have dreamt of such a face, or could it be that amongst one's acquaintance an expression like that was to be found, only in an undeveloped stage? I can remember quite distinctly how that last thought flashed across my mind as I stood hesitating whether to run for bare life, or to wait for some further development of the situation. I think that nothing but the shame of manhood kept me from running away. Just then I suddenly perceived that the men were under some strange and very comprehensive system of drill. The man who seemed to be their leader held them, to all appearance, under very close control. And yet it seemed also as if their submission to his control were voluntary. It was like the way of a very perfect chorus with its conductor. Every glance of the leader's eye, every motion of his hand seemed to affect and direct them. But it did not seem as if there were anything absolutely compulsory about their obedience. They seemed not only to follow his eye and his hand but to look for the guidance of each. The very expression of their faces was moulded upon his, and I could well believe that the malignity which kindled it was kept alive by his.

As I looked more steadily I could see waves of expression, so to speak, going out from his face to them. What particulars these might be conveying I could not guess, but that there were particulars I could not doubt. Their variety, regularity, and distinctive character were as remarkable as if they were spoken words. His hands also moved in harmony with this change of

47

expression, and the bodies of the men swayed with a slight rhythmic movement, which seemed to rise and fall as they watched his changing face. For several seconds I verily thought that I was dreaming, and I even had the feeling that a dreaming man has when he knows that he is about to waken.

Suddenly the leader turned away and the men fell to work as before. I saw then that in his passage along the platform he was encountering group after group of men, and that he was holding with each group, so far as I could guess at the distance, the same sort of silent interview which I have just now described. Then I suddenly remembered my promise to Jack, and I stole away from where I was and ran down the dark passage with breathless haste. Fortunately I received no hurt beyond several scratches in the face from some thorny bushes, which I had not encountered on my way up.

I found Jack very near where I had left him, sleeping under the shadow of a rock. I shook him, and he got up at once, quite broad awake. "Come," I said, "come; I have found men, if they are men." "White men?" he queried, briefly. "God knows," I said, my voice, I believe, quivering with agitation. Jack said no more for the moment, but he gave me a drink of water which I drank very greedily, and he was proceeding leisurely to light his pipe. The water had steadied me a bit, and I said, "No, never mind the pipe now, Jack; I'll tell you as we go along."

So we both went back together over my track, and when we got into the covered way I told him all that I have now told you. Then, when we had got nearly as far as the upper opening of the cave, we sat down and held a short and hurried consultation.

"Let them be what they will," Jack whispered, "we must go straight up and speak to them: if we don't get help soon we shall perish miserably."

"Agreed," I said; "but let us watch them for a little and wait for a favourable moment." And so we both crawled on to the opening of which I have already told you, and looked through.

Everything was just as before, except that the leader was now engaged with a group of men further away. After a brief survey of the surroundings, Jack pulled out his little telescope and looked steadily at the leader and the group of men he was engaged with, and then he handed the glass to me. I could see them with the glass about as plainly as I had seen the near group with the naked eye. Everything was the same, except that the malignant expression of the men and their leader was much less easily recognisable. I handed back the glass, and we both by one impulse drew back from the opening.

48

We drew further back still into a dark and retired corner, quite out of the rough pathway, and held a brief conference.

"It's a queer start," Jack said, "but we must go on with it; it is our only chance."

"It's queerer than you think," said I; "you haven't seen the fellows' faces as I saw them at first."

"No, no, I am taking account of that," said he. "I saw what you mean, although I might not have taken much notice of it if you had not mentioned it. I am afraid they are a very bad lot, or I should say rather he is a bad lot, for they are mere puppets in his hands."

"Not quite that," said I. "I don't suppose they would be much without him, but they are following him with a will."

"That may be," he replied; "but now tell me, how shall we work it? We have no time to lose, for he knows we are coming."

"I don't see how he could know it," said I, "unless he is the devil himself."

Jack gave a short but unpleasant chuckle; then he said,

"Well, perhaps he is; he is bad enough to be, or else I am much mistaken. Anyway, he knows we are coming; that is why the malignant look is partly hidden; he is getting ready for us."

I wished for the light that I might see Jack's face, for his voice began to have an odd ring about it. Then I said, "What can he want with us, Jack?"

"I don't know," he said, "but I made a study of his face just now. I'm not much on—what do you call it?—physiognomy? but that beggar's face told me a story."

"What was the story?"

"Well, that he knows we are coming, and that he wants us, and that he is going to make use of us. What are we going to do?"

"We will go straight up to him and ask him to help us."

"Very well," Jack said. "Rest, and a guide, and food, and fire. And what story shall we tell him of ourselves?"

"We will tell him the truth," said I.

"And shame the devil," said he, with another uncomfortable chuckle.

"What language shall I try him with?" said I.

"Bet you a pound he knows English," said Jack.

"Oh, that's the sort of devil you think he is; very well, I'll take your bet, though I dare say you are right enough." I declare, although I knew very well what ruffians outlawed Englishmen are apt to be, I felt quite light-hearted as I thought that perhaps after all the men we were going to meet might be no worse than such. "Come on," I said, and we walked straight to the light. I pulled aside the

49

rustic frame, which came with my hand quite easily; then I walked straight through, Jack following me closely.

The strange leader saw us at once, stood still, and looked at us. We walked forward and saluted him. I felt at the moment that Jack was right, that he knew that we were coming, although he wore an air of surprise, interested and self-possessed. I thought at the very first, "After all, he looks noble." But almost immediately I changed the word "noble" for "very strong."

He spoke to us in English. I looked at Jack, who smiled grimly and whispered, "Lost, old man." The strange leader said,

"Who are you, and whence do you come?" He spoke perfectly, quite perfectly, and in a commanding and confident tone. But there was a something, I know not what, about his accent, which told me that he was speaking a language foreign to him, and then and afterwards I noticed also that he did not use the conversational idiomatic English of any of those who speak English as their mother tongue.

"We are Englishmen," I said, "and we come from the eastward. We went among the blacks and they left us, and we do not know our way. Can you give us food and clothes, and guide us to the nearest English settlement?"

"I can give you both food and clothes," he said; "about guidance we shall speak farther when you have made up your mind whither your purpose is to go."

I was about to thank him when I suddenly noticed the aspect of his men. They were looking at us eagerly, and it seemed as if they were waiting for some expected word of command. I could not help thinking that they were about to spring upon us, and I put my hand instinctively to the pocket where I kept my pistol.

The leader said shortly, "Never mind that." Then he turned to his men. I could not see his face, but I saw that he lifted his hand. Presently the men were working away at their previous work, and were taking no more note at all of us.

"Come with me," said the leader, and he walked down the broad stone stairway. It was a very broad stairway, with stone balustrades on each side, light in appearance, but immensely strong. Every step, as well as the whole of the balustrade, was diversified with a variety of pictures and devices wrought upon stone by some method which rendered them proof against the weather. On this occasion I noticed little but the colours, but I observed them very closely afterwards. They appeared not only here, but everywhere in the valley, whether under cover or in the

50

open air, wherever there was any space to receive them, on walls, floors, ceilings, pillars, and doors.

All these pictures and devices presented one pervading idea; and as one passed backward and forward over steps and through doors, past pillars and balustrades, and walls, this idea gradually wrought its way into one's mind, until it seemed to dominate, or at least to claim to dominate everywhere. The idea so presented was that of an unequal but very determined conflict. Sometimes there was a simple device, a heavy drawn sword, for one, falling sheer, a cloud hiding the arm that sped it, and a gauntleted hand raised in resistance. This hand was but small and slight as compared with the sword, but there was expression in every sinew of it and in its very poise.

Again, you would see a hand coming out of a cloud and wielding a flash of lightning, and underneath two smaller hands lifted up as if trying to catch the extremities of the zigzag line of light. But the eeriest of all the devices was that of the two eyes: the larger eye was above and the lesser beneath, and how such expression could be given to an eye by itself I do not understand, but certainly there it was. Either eye was looking steadfastly into the other, and in the upper eye you saw conscious power, harsh, stern, and unrelenting; and in the lower and lesser one you saw, quite as plainly, the spirit of hopeless but unquelled resistance. The same idea was repeated in many pictures. In one of them you saw a great host bearing down upon a few antagonists of determined if despairing aspect. And in the background a dark mass of cloud, forest, and rock hid all but the forefront of the mightier combatants and gave you the notion of unseen and inscrutable power. Still, the simpler devices, I think, suggested with more awful certainty the actual presence of desperate and deadly struggle.

As I have said, however, I was conscious of but little of all this as I walked down the broad stone stair. I was weary, and hungry, and thirsty, and utterly taken by surprise, and I was quite ready to attribute to these feelings the sense of eeriness and fear which was creeping over me.

Our host conducted us down the stair with stately courtesy, and he gave us briefly to understand that he was about to ask us to refresh ourselves with food and rest and change of raiment. At the foot of the stair a very broad roadway led straight on toward the other end of the valley, but our host beckoned us to the right by a shorter and narrower way. We entered one of the low buildings which I had seen from above. These were not very large, but they proved to be considerably larger than I had supposed. We passed through a little porch into a fair-sized room, the floor of which was covered with a stuff of curious texture. It looked like some sort of metal; it felt beneath the feet like the softest pile. The walls on one side of the room exhibited a number of drawers with handles. Both drawers and handles were of strange and irregular shapes, exhibiting, nevertheless, a sort of regular recurrence in their very irregularities. In the centre of each of the remaining walls was a picture wrought upon the surface of the wall and occupying about a third of the whole wall, and over the rest of the wall there was inscribed a variety of devices. Both picture and devices were of the sort which I have already indicated.

There was an elliptical table in the middle of the room, and here and there on the floor were several chairs and a few couches, all of a very bizarre pattern, and all—tables, couches, chairs, drawers, and floorcloth—were covered with devices, some similar in form and all similar in spirit to those upon the wall. In the wall opposite the drawers there was a door, and our host, opening this, showed us into a room of lesser size where there were all sorts of appliances for bathing and for dressing. Clothes also, like those worn by himself and his men, hung round on racks. The walls and furniture, here as well as elsewhere, presented repetitions under various forms of the same pictured idea.

Before taking us into the bath-room, our host pulled out three drawers, calling our attention to the numbers marked upon them. Out of each he took a number of little round cakes or lozenges, each of a little less than the circumference of a two-shilling piece, but rather thicker. These he placed on several dishes, a different sort on each dish, and two spoons, or like spoons, on each dish also. He told us to take each, after the bath, a few of these, and he told us in what order we were to take them. Then, with a salutation, he left us to ourselves.

We bathed quickly, and after our bath we availed ourselves gladly of the change of raiment which our host had placed at our disposal. We exchanged a very few words, and those few did not attempt to deal with the mystery which was thickening about us. Jack's face expressed a mixture of surprise and mistrust, each in an extreme degree. My own face, as Jack told me later on, expressed sheer bewilderment. Certainly that was my feeling until far into the middle of the next day. I did not really believe that I was awake and in my senses, and I kept going back and back in my thoughts trying to find out when and where I fell asleep or was stunned.

After our bath we returned into the larger room. We were then very hungry, and we lay down each upon a couch, expecting to be soon summoned to the evening meal, for by this time the afternoon was well advanced. The weather was pleasantly warm, and we would have dropped asleep if we had not been kept awake by hunger. We both remembered at the same moment the plates of confections which our host had offered us. We took first one and then another of each kind in the order which he had indicated, letting them slowly melt in our mouths. The taste of them, although pleasant, was rather strange, but yet not altogether unfamiliar. The taste of the first sort faintly resembled the taste of roast beef; of the second, of pine-apple; of the third, of sweet wine, specially of muscatel. The effect of them was extraordinary; we felt that we had partaken of an agreeable and substantial meal; our hunger and thirst were gone, and we were quite refreshed. And then, as will happen when one dines well after a laborious and exciting day, we both fell sound asleep. We slept all through the night and on until a little after sunrise, and, not to go into details, we rose immediately and breakfasted as we had dined. We had scarce finished our meal when we became aware of the tramp of many men at no great distance from us, and we hurried to the door. We saw then, what neither of us had noticed the evening before, that the broad road, out of which we had turned in order to reach our present resting-place, opened out at the distance of about two hundred yards from the flight of steps into a large square, formed as the road itself was formed, and planted around the borders with trees, under the shade of which were several benches.

In the square were some two or three hundred men, undergoing some sort of review by the leader, with whom we had already become acquainted. Whatever degree of mistrust either of us felt we thought it as well not to show it, so we came forward leisurely until we were within a few score paces of the men, and then we stood and looked. We were not at once perceived, as neither the leader nor his men were looking straight in our direction, and we were partly shaded by a tree. The men were evidently of a much higher stamp intellectually than those whom we had seen the day before, excepting the leader. The men, yesterday, seemed to differ from automatic machines in one single point, namely, that they seemed to have a will of their own, although they had surrendered it to their leader. They seemed, you would say, quite incapable of action except as prompted by him, although they gave themselves up to his prompting, no doubt, because of sympathy and unity of purpose with him. The men to-day seemed, on the contrary, to be men of considerable intelligence. You would suppose them to be quite capable of being leaders themselves, and able to carry out in

53

full detail instructions which they might receive in the merest outline. It was evident that they were now receiving instructions. These were being given, partly by expressions and signs, and partly by some spoken language. The language, which I heard several times in the next two days, bore no resemblance at all to any language that I knew. It seemed to be very artificial and elliptical. The former quality was suggested by the regular recurrence and gradation of certain sounds, and the latter quality was suggested by its great brevity. A word or two seemed to suffice where we should require one or more sentences.

When the leader had given his instructions, one and another, and then another, of the men stood out from the ranks and spoke to him, and in each case he replied. The men who spoke I judged to be in some subordinate command. All the men stood in files now, one man behind another, facing the leader, and in each case the man who spoke stood in front of his file. These files formed themselves quite suddenly and with great precision after the leader had given his first orders and before the other men spoke. It seemed as if the subordinate leaders were making suggestions or inquiries respecting the details of the work about which they had just received instructions in outline.

Then followed what seemed like a numbering of the men, and it soon became apparent that one file had two men missing, that is to say, supposing all the files to have been at first equal in number. As the deficiency became apparent a flash of baffled but furious malignity passed across the leader's face. Then I knew that when I had seen the like expression yesterday I was not dreaming. Jack and I exchanged a momentary glance. Some words, as I judged of inquiry and unsatisfactory reply, passed between the leader and one of his subordinates, and then, in the progress of the drill, the men made a partial turn by which they brought us into full view. In a moment they saw us, and in a moment the same eager and threatening look came over their faces which we had seen in the other men's faces yesterday. Jack and I both believed for that moment that our last hour was come.

But the leader withheld them with a word and a sign. What he said or signified of course I did not really know, but I felt sure, nevertheless, that it was to this effect, that we should supply the places of their comrades who had disappeared. The same thought occurred to Jack. His word was received with a sound like a laugh, but it was a very horrible and ghastly laugh. One sometimes hears of the horror of a maniac's laugh; but the maniac's laugh is horrible by reason of its vacancy. This laugh was by no means vacant, it was full of expression, but it was the expression of relentless malignity.

Then the leader dismissed the men and they moved away towards the further end of the valley. Then he turned and moved slowly towards us and we moved slowly to meet him. He met us with the same stately courtesy as before and we exchanged salutations. He led us to the square where the men had been and he invited us to sit down. Then he inquired briefly concerning our personal comfort and we both expressed briefly our thanks and satisfaction. Then I went on to say,

"My name, sir, is Easterley, and my friend is Mr. Wilbraham, and we have only now to ask you by what name we are to know our host, and to ask that he will add to the obligation under which he has placed us, by giving us a guide to the nearest station or settlement of English colonists."

"I have more names than one," he replied, "among your people, but when I was last in Italy, which is a country that I know better than most, I was known as Niccolo Davelli. I was an analytical chemist and something of an engineer, and I did, well, a little political work among the country folk." He said all this with a very easy manner but with a very unpleasant smile. "Signor Davelli," I replied, speaking in Italian, "I am proud to thank you by name on behalf of myself and my friend, and I trust you will find no difficulty in giving the guidance we ask." "Surely not," he answered in the same language, "but you will stay here for a little, will you not? I have some curious things to show you, and you may perhaps meet some old friends among my people, and my work is so interesting and important that I have some hope that you will see your way to cast in your lot with us altogether. But," said he, "you need not use Italian, for I am not any more skilful in that than in your own equally famous tongue." Here again was the unpleasant smile, and I noticed that although he spoke Italian, as far as I could judge quite perfectly, he used this language as well as English with the deliberate and measured enunciation of a foreigner.

"As you will," I replied, returning to English, "we shall be glad to see what you have to show us."

Signor Davelli rose up at the word and invited us to follow him. He went up the stair by which we had come down the day before, and led us to the platform on which we had first seen him. He told us briefly that his sojourn here was in fulfilment of a purpose to which he and certain others of his fellowship were pledged. That they were all acting in concert and that certain of them were leaders, and that each leader had command of a station such as this, of which there were several in different parts of the world. That it was essential to the work that it should be carried on from regions far removed from the haunts of men, at least of civilised men, for they could repel the interference of savage races without endangering the fulfilment of their purpose. He went on to tell us that in this station of his he had two classes of work to do, one class consisting of intellectual work of a high order, and affecting more directly the fulfilment of the common purpose, the other class consisting of merely mechanical work, affecting the routine of life and its conditions here. "The men," he went on to say, "who carry out the former are of high and independent mental faculties and rank accordingly; these men you have seen to-day. The men who carry out the latter are of a very acute capacity to receive and execute instructions, but have no originating power of conception or design. These are they whom you saw yesterday. Their work is mainly the making of our food and clothes, and the construction of our means of locomotion, and of the machinery by which the work is done. That machinery is designed and executed in model at the other end of the valley by the other men in the intervals of their more important work. That work, however, you cannot understand until you become better acquainted with us."

We had now reached the platform, and we saw the men at work just as we had seen them the day before. Signor Davelli uttered a single word which I did not understand, and on hearing it the men turned, and then followed for a very few minutes the same sort of pantomimic action which I had already seen and have described. Then they resumed work.

Signor Davelli then took us to the works and invited us to observe the construction of the various machines in use.

I must not, however, run the risk of tiring you by any minute account of them here. Let it suffice to say that there was a much higher degree of mechanical skill exhibited in their construction than I have ever seen anywhere before or since, and that besides there was much that suggested the application of chemical and electrical science in a manner greatly in advance of anything that is commonly known; and further that there were certain complicated arrangements of prisms and mirrors which indicated as I thought some use of the agency of light which was quite new to me and which I did not understand. One set of machines proved to be used for the manufacture of the compressed food which we had already found so effective. Another set of much simpler construction carried it away and stored it when made. Yet another set was used for the manufacture of that invisible paint, the use of which had so astonished me. These last were the machines which attracted my curiosity most of all, and which implied not only a use which I did not comprehend of agencies which I recognised, but the existence of other agencies of which I knew nothing at all. I observed, however, as carefully as possible and I made, later on, very full notes of what I did observe, and I shall be happy to communicate these to our men of science in whose hands they can hardly fail to become of much practical value. I need hardly say that I asked a good many questions about this last set of machines, but somehow I got very little information. Whether Signor Davelli was unwilling to explain, or whether there was something in the process which I was incapable of understanding, I am not quite sure. All I could get from him was that there are some rays at either end of the spectrum which are not visible, and that it is possible to treat some substances so as to cause them to reflect these rays only, just as other substances reflect only the yellow or only the red. But from a word or two which he spoke, I suspect inadvertently, I gathered that the rays he spoke of, which are invisible to us, were visible to him, and differed as much from yellow, red, or blue, as these from one another.

We now crossed the platform to the place where the cars were being painted. I perceived as soon as I came upon the spot that the cars were built at one level, and then raised by machinery to another level at which they were painted, and that when painted they were raised to a third level. Along each of these levels they were moved by rollers of quite simple construction. Yesterday I had only seen those on the second level; those on the first were too low to come within the field of my view, and those on the third were invisible.

On this third level, however, one was to-day visible. As I afterwards learned, Signor Davelli had caused it to be left unpainted. It was otherwise finished. He caused it now to be rolled along to the extremity of the platform, which ended to the southward in a sheer precipice of some hundreds of feet. There was a ledge to keep it from rolling over. Signor Davelli led us to this car and invited us to enter it.

There was plenty of accommodation for two or three people. There were easy benches and couches, and there were three boxes with distinctive marks like numbers on the lids. At the end of the car which was furthest from the ledge, the inside end, there was a great deal of machinery, but not of such a size as I should have expected considering the size of the car. This machinery consisted of two batteries resembling galvanic batteries in many ways, but the stuff used up in work was not fluid but solid; it consisted of large squares of matter, which I think was wholly or mainly metallic. The batteries were connected with a strong round bar, made, as I thought, of some sort of metal[3] running through the car and supporting a pair of huge paddles, or wings, one on each side of the car. At each end of the bar were certain little wheels and cranks, devised not so as to cause the paddles to revolve, but so as to give them a wing-like motion. At the forward part of the car were several vessels of a form which suggested a chemical apparatus for generating gas. And on each side of the car, constructed and placed with an evident view to balance or trim it, were two balloons, which seemed absurdly small in view of the size of the car. These were connected with the chemical apparatus just mentioned, and were filled by it, when occasion required, with a gas vastly lighter than hydrogen.

Signor Davelli, Jack, and I entered the car, and the Signor took a bottle of liquid out of one of the numbered boxes and poured it into one of the vessels. Then in all the vessels there seemed to be a sound like boiling, and presently the balloons became inflated and raised the car very gently and quite evenly. When we had been thus lifted to a height of about a hundred feet from the platform, he put on a dark-looking pair of gloves and laid hold of a strong thick wire, which I had not seen before, which was fastened to the bar which I had supposed to be of metal on the side further from where I sat. This wire he connected with the batteries of either end, and immediately took off the gloves. Presently the paddles began to move with a wing-like action, driving the car straight forward through the air. All this time we were still rising slowly, but when we had attained a high degree of speed Signor Davelli turned the key of a valve which communicated with both balloons and they presently collapsed, the action of the paddles being now sufficient both to sustain us and to urge us forward. The motion was easier than that of any conveyance that I had ever yet travelled in. The seat on which Signor Davelli sat was placed so that with one hand he could turn the key of the valve, and with the other grasp either of two handles, by one of which he managed the batteries, and by the other of which he changed at need the direction of the paddles. I perceived, upon looking more closely, that the key of the valve was fixed at the intersection of two tubes shaped like a T, one at right angles to the other, the horizontal tube joining the balloons and the perpendicular tube connected with the vessels from which the sound of boiling still proceeded.

After we had gone, as I thought, a few miles, Signor Davelli changed the direction of the paddles and swept round in a longish curve, until the forward part of the car was turned to our starting

---

[3] I discovered afterwards that it was not metallic.

point. When we had travelled about half way back he turned the valve again and refilled the balloons, and then he stopped the paddles and we lay floating in the air, rising very slowly and gently. Then he bade me look to the west and say if I saw anything. I could see nothing at all, the day was quite cloudless. Then he bade me look downward, but still to the west. Then I saw a shadow, as I thought, of a great bird, but I could see no bird to cast the shadow. The sun was now declining a little, and he bade me turn and look downward again, but now to the east. Then I saw the shadow of our own car, and although the point of view was not the same, there was no room to doubt but that the other shadow was cast by a car like ours. The moment I saw the likeness my old Welsh experience came with a flash to my mind. These were just the same queer sort of shadows that I had seen long ago at Penruddock the day James Redpath had disappeared; yes, and surely the evening before the day we reached the valley, the evening of the day that we lost poor Gioro I had seen just the same sort of shadow. And—— Could it be? Yes, it surely was—the dreadful face that I recognised yesterday was no other than James Redpath's own! How it was that I did not identify him before I do not know, but now I knew very surely that I had seen himself indeed. Such was the tumult of mixed feelings that now took possession of me that although we moved rapidly forward again until we had passed quite over the valley and then wheeled round once more, I took no notice of our movements until I found that we were descending to the spot where we had started, the front of the car facing southward as before. I looked at Signor Davelli, and I read in his face an expression of gratified pride and a strong sense of power. There was nothing repulsive in his aspect now, at least nothing repulsive to me. I felt also that I was being somehow dominated by his will, and that I was not altogether unwilling that it should be so. I felt certainly some remnant of the horror with which I had looked yesterday on his face and the faces of his men, but I was conscious that my horror was rapidly merging into simple wonder. I felt something of the sort of awe which the suspected presence of the supernatural produces in most minds; but the feeling which dominated for the present all other feelings in me was a devouring curiosity. Just then the sacred allegory of the Fall passed before my mind rather as if presented than recalled. In my mind's eye I saw the very Tree itself which was to be desired to make one wise, and the legend written under it—

"Eritis sicut Deus scientes bonum et malum;"

59

but neither device nor motto seemed to have any other effect upon me than to stimulate my curiosity.

Just then we touched ground, and I started, as if coming to my senses, and looked over at Jack. His face was partly turned away, and I could see little more than his side face. He wore an abstracted air, such as I had never seen him wear before. There was also a sweetness and earnestness of expression about him which were certainly not foreign to his face, but which I had never before seen there in such intense degree. Strange to say, there came upon me for the moment a sort of contempt for his understanding which seemed strongly to repel me from him. This, I have now no doubt, was produced by some evil influence acting I know not how, for assuredly there was nothing in my knowledge of him that it could build upon, and all that happened after justified it, if possible, even less. Just then he turned and looked upon me, and there was in his eyes so much care and kindness, kindness to me and care on my account, that my heart was touched and awakened at once. I cannot analyze or account for the effect which this look produced on me; I can only say that as I stepped from the car the tumult of mixed feelings, which so disturbed me, seemed to pass away like a bad dream that might or might not return.

After a few words of courteous inquiry as to our necessities and comforts, Signor Davelli made an appointment to meet us next day on the square where we had met this morning; and then we parted from him for the night, and Jack and I slowly returned to our place.

"Jack," said I, as we were going down, "what do you think of it all?"

"We won't talk of it now," he replied, "we are too tired, and perhaps excited; we had better sleep over it. To-morrow we must rise early, look out a quiet place, and talk the matter all round."

Nothing more but some words of course passed between us until the morning.

CHAPTER VIII

SIGNOR DAVELLI

Early the next morning Jack and I were ready for a scramble over the cliff. We wished to have a quiet talk together, and we wished farther, although we had not yet named the wish one to another, to ascertain as far as possible whether or not we were in effect prisoners. There was one fact which told heavily against any such notion. That was the large quantity of portable provisions which had been deliberately put in our way. For we could each carry, without inconvenience, enough to last us for a long time, quite long enough to enable us to push westward as far as the coast, or to go back eastward as far as the wire. Nevertheless, I was firmly of opinion that we would not be permitted to escape, and that if we attempted to our lives would not be worth much. As I learned afterwards, Jack was of the same opinion. The events of this morning removed all doubt on the subject.

We found quite a practicable ascent of the cliff on the side of the stair which was further from the platform. And, after climbing this, we found a fairly even space of several hundred yards, and then an easy descent upon the other side. We did not, however, attempt the descent, but sat down and talked. Jack began—

"Bob," he said, "we must keep cool, for we are playing for very high stakes."

"For life and death, you think."

"More than that, perhaps. I wonder what selling your soul meant in the old times?"

"I suppose," I said, "whatever else it meant, it meant acting dishonourably or treacherously for the sake of some personal gain."

"But some fellows have sold their souls who could never be persuaded to act either treacherously or dishonourably for the sake of any personal gain."

"I daresay," said I, not seeing nor caring what he was driving at.

"Now, Bob, if I were the devil, and if I wanted to get you to sell me your soul, I know what I should do."

I was getting a little vexed, but I replied simply—"Well, what would you do?"

"I would endeavour to pique your curiosity, and then I would

61

show you that you could gratify it by putting yourself in my power, and then I would have your body even if you still insisted on keeping your soul."

"And which do you think it would be?"

"Well, I should have to be satisfied with your body, except in one event."

"And, pray, what would that be?"

"I might by the exhibition of some special or unaccounted-for power gain such influence over you as to get you to put your conscience at my disposal. Then you would be mine soul and body."

I was beginning to get vexed, partly because I suppose I saw more truth in what he said than I liked, so I said shortly—

"What do you mean just now by all this?"

"I think our friend, the signor, is the devil himself. I don't mean any fee-faw-fum. I daresay there are a good many other men as much devils as he is, but he has all the power which great and special practical knowledge gives a man, and he is as full of malice as an egg is full of meat, and he is up to some very big villainy and, what is more to the purpose, he has a design upon you."

"He has done us no harm that I can see."

"He has done us a great deal of harm; he is persuading you to trust yourself to him, and he is worthy of no trust whatever, d—n him."

Now this from Jack was rather startling; for he was not in the least prone to use bad language. I never heard "the Englishman's prayer" from his lips before or since. But his earnestness irritated me more than his profanity surprised me.

"Don't you see," I said rather sullenly, "that if your hypothesis is correct your prayer is rather superfluous?"

"Well, yes, it is superfluous," he said with a harsh laugh quite unlike him; "he is damned already sure enough."

"I don't see much sign of damnation about him," I said, "not if misery be an essential part of damnation."

"Well, yes, the misery that comes of malice, and if ever malice and misery were written in a man's face, they were written in his yesterday when they missed those men. And mark me," Jack added, raising his voice, "his damnation has got something to do with the loss of those men."

I was now getting very angry, so I rose to my feet and said hastily—"If we have nothing to talk about, don't you think that we may as well go back?"

Jack rose and said, "No, Bob, we'll not go back yet awhile. Don't be vexed with me, old fellow. You are in more danger than I am, but your danger is mine." As he said this I saw the same expression on his face which I had seen yesterday, an expression of kindness and anxiety, and it had much the same effect on me now.

"Jack," I said, "forgive me, I declare I believe you are partly right; I believe there is some devilish influence at work trying to set me against you. I caught myself yesterday despising you for not being clever, and there were two devils in that, for you are twice as clever as I am, and even if you were not you are ten times as good."

"Ah, Bob, my boy, there is plenty of reason to suspect me of stupidity without supposing that the devil is in the dance.

'Nec deus (or diabolus) intersit nisi dignus vindice nodus.'

You see I have a stock verse or two to quote at a pinch. But although I don't see as far, perhaps, into the game as you, it may be that just for that reason I see the near points a little more clearly. Now sit down again and tell me what you think of it all."

We didn't sit but kept walking up and down. "I don't know what to think," I said; "I was nearly sure yesterday that I was either mad or dreaming, but I have given over thinking that. I suppose there is a desperate and widely spread conspiracy against civilised society, and that these men are in it. You talk about fee-faw-fum, but I remembered some things yesterday while we were in that car that made me feel as if the whole world were nothing but what you call fee-faw-fum."

"What were they, Bob?"

I told him all that I have written in the first two chapters of this book. He listened most attentively, and made me repeat two or three times over parts of the conversation between the two doctors. But when I wound up my story by telling him that I had recognised James Redpath among the men on the platform, he stopped suddenly, turned right round and looked at me. "Good heavens!" he said. And then after a pause, "Do you think that you saw him carried away that morning from your Welsh village?"

"I didn't see him, but I have little doubt that I saw the shadow of the car in which he was carried away."

"Do you think that we have stumbled on your friend Dr. Leopold's non-human intelligence? and that there is a manufactory of black death or plague somewhere in the neighbourhood?"

"I have hardly a doubt of these men's malignity, but there is one thing I am surer of. Now that I am here I want to know all about the matter—and I mean to. Mr. Leopold may have stumbled upon half a truth."

"Well, my position is just the reverse of yours. I am curious enough about the matter, but I am so sure of these men's desperate malignity that my first wish is that we should make our escape from this place. And mind," he went on to say, "if you want to burst them up that is the way to do it. If you and I get back to civilisation others will soon be on our track. And once there is a settlement of English colonists near here these men will be played out, and they know it. Don't you remember what the fellow himself said? He said that they could keep the blacks at a distance, but that it does not suit them to carry on their work—whatever it is—in the presence of civilised men!"

"I remember," said I; "but if you are right, depend upon it they have made up their minds that you and I will never leave this place alive."

"Not quite that," said he, "or they would have murdered us before now."

"Well, they were going to do so twice."

"Yes, but Signor Niccolo restrained them. You see Signor Niccolo has a design upon you; he wants to make you one of his men. He doesn't care much about me, but he is willing to throw me into the bargain. Now if you and I refuse to join him our lives will be the forfeit."

"And if we don't refuse?"

"Why then," said he, "more than our lives."

"Well then," said I, "what in the name of common sense do you think they are?"

"Well," he replied, "I don't altogether agree with Dr. Leopold. I can't quite believe in the 'non-human' business; these men are flesh and blood safe enough; though I confess I am startled to see so much applied science, so much in advance of ours, in the possession of men of such malignity as these are." He paused for a moment and then proceeded. "What you said just now is most likely right. They belong most likely to some brotherhood of conspirators, some advanced guard of Nihilists, or the like, who propose to make war upon civilised society."

"What do you advise?"

"For all reasons the sooner we get away the better. My proposition is that we fill our pockets with these cakes of theirs and make a bolt of it the very first opportunity."

"Do you think we shall find an opportunity?"

"Well, the event will show. We may have to start in the dark and for a while to travel by night. But you see these cakes of theirs are meat and drink, and we can make a bee-line for the wire."

64

"Don't you think they will track us?"

"I doubt if they will be able. Their intelligence is very high, and their modes of procedure are very artificial; and the best trackers are men of mere instinct. Still I wish we could get hold of one of their cars; if we could, a few hours' start would save us."

"Look to the right," I said, "we are watched and followed now."

By this time the sun had risen a little way, the sky was clear, and here and there, slowly moving along the face of the cliff below us, were several shadows of the sort I have already more than once described. These plainly indicated the presence of several of the cars at no great distance from the ground, and at a lower level than the cliff on which we stood. Whether there were any or how many at a higher level no one could say just yet, and on the left everything lay still in shadow. We walked in the same direction, quickening our steps a little, the cliff all the while sloping downward slowly. Presently the sun was at a higher level than the ground we walked on, and the number of the shadows greatly increased, and there were very many now on all sides of us. Just then it seemed as if a cloud were passing over us quite near. We looked upward quickly, but there was no cloud, only a great shadow cast, as it would seem, by nothing. In a few seconds it was gone, and presently after we heard the swish—sh—sh right over us of the wing-like paddles, and we could even detect the small regular rattle of the machinery. It was evident that we were being closely guarded, and perhaps we were overheard.

Silently but with one impulse we turned and walked slowly back to the rooms that had been assigned to us.

We refreshed ourselves with food and we had an hour's rest before it was time to keep our appointment with our host. We agreed meanwhile to observe everything very closely and to compare notes at night.

"But," said I, "is it safe for us to separate?"

"Nothing, of course," Jack answered, "is altogether safe, but for a little while I think that we are not in any more danger apart than together."

"But you know, Jack, you said that you thought he had some special design on me and that he didn't want you. So he may have you quietly put out of the way if you go alone."

"He is bad enough for anything," was the answer, "but he knows that to put me out of the way would so disturb you as to baffle his designs upon you. Your attention would be entirely diverted from the matters in which you are now taking so deep an interest, and by means of which he hopes to secure you. He would have to put you out of the way too, and he doesn't want to do that. So he is going, as I have said, to throw me into the bargain."

"What course do you suggest then, when we are next left to ourselves?"

"You try to get an interview with—what's his name?—your old Welsh friend?"

"James Redpath."

"Just so, and I will try to pick up some information about the navigation of the cars."

At the appointed hour, which was rather early in the afternoon, we went together to the square, and we had hardly reached it when Signor Davelli arrived there too. His appearance was decidedly changed: his robe was ampler and longer, and this as well as his hat and sandals were apparently made of richer and lighter stuff than those which he had worn before, also there were various mottoes and devices wrought upon them. The devices were all of the sort I have before told you of, and the mottoes, or what I deemed such, were in a variety of characters, most of them altogether unknown to me. A few of them, however, were in languages that I knew. There was only one in English, and strange to say, I cannot remember what it was. On the front of the hat was an inscription in Hebrew characters, but so oddly formed that I did not at first recognise them. I am not much skilled in Hebrew but I have no doubt that the inscription was כאלהים[4] written, however, in a character closely resembling that of the Palmyra inscriptions. As I came slowly to recognise the meaning of this inscription, it came to me much more forcibly (and with another sort of force), than if I had at once recognised it for what it was. And I would have at once recognised it if it had been in the ordinary square characters as I have written it here.

Signor Davelli's manner was, as I thought, very stately and even majestic, and yet at the same time quite easy and affable. Once or twice only I observed an air of effort, and even that seemed as of an effort graciously undertaken even if painful. Once or twice also a sort of spasm crossed his face as of self-repression of some sort. And once it seemed as if he were about to spring forward but checked himself, and his face then reminded me of the faces of his men yesterday in this very square when they first recognised our presence.

---

4 "As gods." Gen. iii. 5.

He bade us be seated, and he took a seat himself and began to talk to us. Our seats faced his and there was a pathway like a garden walk between us. I remember noticing as he began to speak that the same strange flowers and shrubs which I had seen outside grew in great abundance along this pathway.

Signor Davelli led the conversation quickly, but not at all with violence, to themes of an abstract character, and he presently settled down to the discussion of no less a subject than free will.

You would not thank me if I were to give you (supposing I could do so) a full account of all that he said. I will, therefore, not make any such attempt. I will only say that his remarks were bold and interesting, although he presented no aspect of the question which was absolutely new to me, and that he spoke apparently with strong feeling and fervour, and even sometimes with a bitter air of desperation. Then he looked at me with an air of inquiry.

After a long pause I said,

"I see, Signor Davelli, that you are not a materialist."

"Materialist?" he said, with a very unpleasant mixture of smile and sneer. "No; materialism is very well for a beginning; but one must face the facts at last if one is to deal with them at all successfully."

"But," said I, "some teach that matter is the very ultimate of all fact."

"It is perhaps well," he said, with a renewal of the same sneer and smile, "that they should teach so, but you and I know better; matter is evidence of the fact, but not the fact itself."

"And free will in your view is real?"

"Yes, it is real, doubtless, although so given as to make it for all but the very boldest practically unreal."

"So given, you say; it is a gift then?"

"Yes, it is a gift, if you call that 'given' which you use at your peril."

"And who gives it?" said I.

"Never mind that," he said, with a bitter scowl, which recalled for the moment his malignant expression of the day but one before. "Call Him the Giver: a cursed way of giving is His. You know that you can use His gift if you dare, and you know that if you dare use it as you please He will scald you with what His bond-slaves call 'the vials of His wrath'; that I think is the phrase."

"Perhaps," I said, "the scalding is one's own doing: power to use the gift is power to use it rightly or wrongly: if one choose to use it wrongly one takes the consequences."

"Right and wrong," he said, "what are they?" and he spoke

67

now with great coolness and without a sign of sneer; "trace back the ideas to their origin. Right is what I will, and wrong is what I will not. So it is with the Giver, and why should it not be so with you and me?" I observed that as he said this some of the mottoes on his dress grew bright and even flashed. Among them was that in Hebrew letters which I told you of just now. "But I know there are slaves," he went on to say, "slaves (you surely are not one of them) who are afraid of liberty, and who are jealous of those who are not afraid of it. And these," he said, and here the scowl returned, "these make use of such words as right and wrong to perpetuate the tyrannous rule of Him who gives with a curse, and who takes again with a fresh curse."

"Is He," I said, "the tyrant on whom you are making war?"

"Oh, yes," he said, "for all tyrants hold from Him; they are His hired bullies whom he pampers and lashes as you might lash and pamper your dog."

"You say that He gives and takes, will He take the gift of the freedom of will from you?"

If I had foreseen the effect which this question would have produced, I should certainly have been afraid to have asked it. His face became at once full of deadly fury and frenzy; "Yes," he said, "curse Him! He will at last if He can!" And then he sprang up and caught at the air with both his hands, just like the hands, in the device of which I have told you, grasping at the forked lightning.

In a moment, however, he resumed the quiet, stately and affable air, which he had worn before, and he sat down, and began to talk again quite calmly.

"Yes," he said, "free will is no doubt real to the bold and desperate spirit. To all others it is in effect unreal. To make it in effect real to all, every free being ought to be able to do as he will, not only without let or hindrance, but also without what you I suppose would call penal consequences."

"It seems to me," I said, "that our little world is too limited for such freedom as you desire. We should speedily come into collision with each other if there were no limit of any sort to our freedom."

"Yes, if your world were the only world."

I did not notice at the time his use of the pronoun "your" for "our." I only replied, "If our world were multiplied a hundred thousand fold, and I can well believe that there may be a hundred thousand such worlds, still the limits of habitable space must ultimately be a limit to freedom so that it cannot be unconditional."

"There are no limits," he said, "to habitable space."

I began to think that he was a very clever madman, and I said nothing.

"For such as you," he continued, "the limit exists, but not for me, nor for such as I."

Now I was sure he was mad, and I still kept silence.

"Nor yet for you," he added, "either, if you have courage enough to overleap the limit."

Now I began to be afraid that the form of mania which affected him was homicidal, and that he would presently require me, as he said, "to overleap the limit." But he rose to his feet with such a collected air, and looked so full of proud intellect and power that I began to change my mind and to think that I was going mad myself.

He spoke again, stretching out his hand, "Space is unlimited, and wherever space is there is a dwelling-place for me. This form in which I live here is but my dress, which I assume when I come to live among you. I can put it off and live in space, I can put it on again and come back to you. See here!"

Both his hands were now stretched upward, and his eyes were fixed on me with a domineering gaze, and mine on him with a mixture of wonder and of dread. Then he looked away straight out into the southern sky.

Suppose now a great mass of metal to be so quickly molten and vaporized that it has no time to fall to the earth as fluid before it rises into the air as gas. That was how it seemed to happen to the body of this extraordinary man. As I looked at him I saw no longer his body, but a great mass of apparently fluid substance, moved with a continuous ripple all through. Then it increased in volume vastly and spread upward like the smoke from an immense furnace. And as it spread it became thinner and finer, and still thinner and finer, until presently there was not the slightest trace of it any longer to be distinguished. How long a time it took to complete this transformation I could not at all guess from my experience of it. As far as my recollection of that goes, it might have occupied hours, but I know from external facts such as the shadows of the trees and the clouds that it could have been little more than five minutes at most, and on comparing notes afterwards with Jack I became inclined to believe that although I had certainly observed a succession of changes the whole transformation and disappearance was practically instantaneous.

Jack and I said not a word, we were both quite stupefied for the moment. Partly recovering ourselves we both walked up to the spot where Signor Davelli had stood, and we saw what seemed to be

69

the remains of the sandals, hat, and coat, which he had worn. Jack took them up one after another, looked at them, and handed them to me. The texture of none of them was in any way destroyed. But they were now wholly colourless, and not the least trace of any letter or device was anywhere to be seen on them.

After the lapse of about ten minutes a slight explosion was heard a little way over our heads, and then a slight vapour appeared in the air very widely spread. Then I saw the same changes as before, but in reverse order. The vapour thickened into smoke, the smoke became condensed into a fluid rapidly rippling throughout. This presently settled down over the spot where the discarded dress was lying, and became solidified; and as I looked I saw Signor Davelli with the same pose and attitude as before his disappearance, and with the same dress bearing the very same inscriptions and devices.

As before, I am inclined to believe that the reappearance and transformation, although presented to me as a succession of changes, were practically instantaneous.

I stood looking at him, transfixed with wonder and horror. He signed to me to sit down; then he sat down himself, and began to speak again quite gently and persuasively. Jack stood for a minute or two as if in hesitation about something; then he, too, sat down and listened.

Signor Davelli. Do not be alarmed, there is no occasion for alarm nor even for surprise. Nothing has been done but what is quite as fully susceptible of explanation as any simple chemical experiment.

Easterley. That can hardly be so. Much even of what we saw yesterday far exceeded any results of experimental science known to me, but I could readily believe it all to be explicable upon principles which I have studied, and which I partly understand. But the experiment which I have just witnessed (if I may call it an experiment) surely implies principles which far transcend any with which I am in the slightest degree acquainted.

Davelli. "Transcend" them, yes, but are nevertheless closely related to them, and are never at variance with them. But I can put you through an experience quite similar to that which I have myself just undergone. You shall judge for yourself then.

He came quite near me, and went on to speak in a tone at once masterful and persuasive.

"You shall experience my power," he said, "and you shall criticise it. I will send you hence and back in quite a little time. You will remember what you see, and you shall compare it with what you know of your own world, and you shall say then whether it is not worth your while to come and join us. If you join us you will know nothing of what you call death, for death cannot touch the dwellers in space."

As he said these last words I felt a shudder pass through me; it reminded me of something, I knew not what, but afterwards I remembered.

"Cannot death touch you?" I said. "Not even when you are dwelling here with us?"

"No," he replied; "anything that would kill you would simply drive us back into space."

I have a very trustworthy instinct as to the truth or falsehood of those who speak to me, and I felt now that Signor Davelli was speaking the truth in this particular, but that he was deceiving me somehow.

"Do you propose," I said, "to send me among the dwellers in space and to fetch me back now?"

I detected just the faintest turn of his eye towards Jack, and as he answered I knew that he was lying, and that if need were he would lie more.

"You cannot acquire at once," he said, "the powers of a dweller in space. But I shall send you out of this world and I will fetch you back, and your journey will help you to acquire the power to become a dweller in space by-and-by."

I distrusted him profoundly and I was not without fear of him. It was fear, however, that I could not easily define. Certainly it was not fear of death, for I felt quite sure that he was not going to kill me. I felt a consuming desire to know all about him, and I was willing to risk much in order to satisfy my desire. I felt also the influence of his masterful will. My distrust of him weighed one way, and the strength of his will the other way, and my lust of knowledge turned the scale.

So I said, "Send me where you will then."

The words were scarce out of my mouth when he raised his hand, and in a moment I lost all power of active motion, and could neither see nor hear, although my consciousness not only remained but became abnormally distinct.

Of course I had never experienced exactly such a state, but I remember once, in my college days, I had mastered a very abstract philosophical discussion, and I lay down on the hearthrug and thought it over until my power of thought seemed to merge into something clearer and fuller, and once later in life I stood on the deck of a ship gazing on the ocean—

71

"Until the sea and sky
Seemed one, and I seemed one with them and all
Seemed one, and there was only one, and time
And space and thought were one eternity."[5]

On both of these occasions I experienced something not unlike the intensely vivid consciousness which I experienced now.

It was mainly a consciousness of expectancy. The events of the last few days seemed to hang before my mind like a semi-transparent veil which was trembling under the action of the hand that was about to withdraw it in order to discover something wonderful behind.

Then I seemed to be borne onward, I knew not whither, with an inconceivably rapid motion. Then again I lay at rest. Then my power of sight returned, and I think my power of hearing, but there was at first nothing to hear. I seemed to be lying on a hard bank within the mouth of a cave not far below the surface of what seemed to be the earth. A light streamed into the cave, and I could see right opposite me a tract of mountain, wild and rugged beyond all description. The light was not diffused except within the cave. The space outside the cave's mouth seemed quite dark, and then the rugged mountain side beyond shone out quite brilliantly. Looking round I saw nothing but barren rock, and I could hear no sound either around or above, but as I moved my head from side to side I heard a sound from beneath as of a dull "thud, thud," and then a sound strangely like whispering voices.

I had been in a sitting position and I had lain back, and so now I looked up into the sky, and, notwithstanding the apparent daylight, I saw the stars quite plainly, and a monstrous moon, a little past the new phase, nearly overhead, with very distinct markings upon it. I watched steadily the markings near the edge, and I saw that they were moving very slowly, like the minute hand of a huge clock. Looking steadily still, I recognised the markings. I was looking at the earth. I could even distinguish some of the coasts and seas and islands, as it seemed to me, quite plainly recognisable. Now I knew where I was and I started to my feet. I had intended to stand up, but the force which I had exerted with that purpose in view made me bound several feet from the ground, so that my head reached beyond the edge of the cave. I felt as if my breath were suddenly stopped, and I fell back gasping to the ground again.

Then I gave myself up for lost, but in a moment sight and

---

[5] "Nay, then, God be wi' you, an you talk in blank verse."—J.W.

hearing again left me, and the strangely vivid consciousness came back. Then I felt a sense of rapid motion, and presently I found myself sitting on the bench with Signor Davelli bending over me and Jack standing by. Immediately I glanced at the shadows round me, and I saw in a moment that my journey, whatever was its nature, had lasted much longer than Signor Davelli's. I knew at once that he had deceived me, that my lust of knowledge was baulked, and that I had been no nearer to his world than I was now.

I cried out, "You have shown me the moon, perhaps in trance, perhaps you have transferred me there. But what of that? You've shown me nothing of the dwellers in space."

"Be quiet," he said, lifting his hand, and again using the same tone, masterful and yet persuasive, "you have done very well for once;" and then he added in a lower and quite different tone, "and so have I."

I never could make you understand the mixture of contending feelings which began to harass me now. No one, I think, could understand it without undergoing it. I was astonished at what had happened to myself, and yet I was grievously disappointed.

Even if I had been sure that I had been actually transferred to the surface of the moon, that would have seemed as nothing to me now. For what I had looked for was a far greater thing. I had long learned to regard the ether which pervades the interplanetary spaces as the hidden storehouse of material out of which the visible worlds are made, and yet the ether is utterly impalpable to any of the senses, and we know of its existence only by roundabout processes of reasoning, and I had been fool enough to believe that I was going to be put in possession of powers of sense which would enable me to examine the ether just as one might examine any of the ordinary material with which we are familiar. I thought I was going to have a near view of the secret forces which lie behind all mechanical, chemical, and electrical action. And what, in view of such a prospect, did I care about seeing the surface of the moon, even if I did really see it? I knew that on the surface of the moon I should only see, under different conditions, the same sort of material as that with which I was already familiar. And I felt sure, or nearly sure, besides, that I had not seen anything but some picture which this wonderful and mysterious being contrived to impress upon my mind.

Besides, I felt sure now that he was deliberately deceiving me, and the sense of horror and repulsion with which he had more or less affected me from the first were now very greatly increased.

73

Besides, I felt that his power over me was great and was growing greater, and I began to doubt if I could ever shake it off.

But, above all—and now for the first time a bitter sense of remorse filled me on account of my own action in respect of him—I saw that I had been paltering with my conscience, and playing with right and wrong, for the sake of mere intellectual attainment. I knew that I had been doing this ever since this man or devil had first spoken to me. And I felt that my own words deliberately spoken but a little while ago had brought my wrong-doing to a crisis. I felt now that when the words, "Send me where you will, then," had passed my lips I had put myself, to what extent I knew not, within the power of one whom I deeply suspected of some horrible plot against humanity.

I must not say that I was overwhelmed by these feelings, for stronger than any of them was the resolve I now made, with the whole force of my being, that I would never again surrender my will to him on any pretext whatever. And yet I felt very nearly in despair, for I could not but seriously doubt if I had now the power to keep this resolve. I feared that I might be like the drunkard who has taken the first glass.

I suppose there is hardly a man anywhere who has never really prayed. And so I think every reader will understand me when I say, that I lifted up my heart to God silently, and on the moment, with far deeper energy and fervour and self-distrust than ever I thought possible before.

Just then I became aware that Signor Davelli's eyes were off me and that he was talking to Jack: his manner to him was quite courteous and gracious. He was, as it seemed, apologising to him.

"You must pardon me," said he; "I am afraid that my interest in your friend's conversation has diverted my attention unduly from my other guest." Then, after a slight pause, he added, "Now I propose to take your friend to-morrow on an aerial journey, to see the other extremity of the valley, and some of the operations there. I can only take one at a time: you will probably like to come again. But, for to-morrow, how shall we provide for your amusement? we shall be back early in the afternoon."

Jack replied civilly, but with an air of indifference which I thought was feigned, "I should be glad of an opportunity of examining some of the curious engines that we have seen yonder." He pointed as he spoke in the direction of the platform.

"Very well," was the reply; "I will see that you have a guide." As he spoke he took an odd-looking little instrument from a pocket at his girdle, and whistled upon it. The resulting sound consisted of a few recurring notes, with a wild, odd strain of music in them.

In a few moments a man appeared. He came from some place towards the further end of the valley, and he was no doubt one of those whom we had seen on this very square the day before. Signor Davelli spoke to the man. "You will meet this gentleman," he said, "here, to-morrow; his name is Mr. Wilbraham. Meet him at whatever hour he pleases, and show him whatever he wishes to see." Then he spoke a few words in the same strange language as before, and accompanied his words with the same sort of action.

Then he turned to me and said, "Will you meet me here at nine o'clock to-morrow, and I will take you to see what we are doing at the further end of the valley?"

I hesitated for a moment, and then I said, "Yes, I will meet you."

Whether my hesitation, or anything in my tone, indicated that I meant not to commit myself to more than to meet him, I cannot say, but as I spoke a scowl passed over his face. It came and went in a moment, and then he said, "Very well," rather curtly, to me. And then, addressing us both in the same gracious manner as before, "And now you are tired," he said, "and it is getting late; I hope you find your quarters convenient and your commissariat sufficient."

We assured him on both points briefly, made our parting salutation, and retired. I may here mention that the salutations which passed between us and him were never anything more than a formal inclination of the head.

Two more facts must be put on record before I close the account of this eventful day.

We met near the foot of the great stairway the man whom I supposed to be James Redpath. He appeared to be engaged in setting right some detail of the machinery made use of by the workers on the platform. I could not but think as I looked upon him that he had all the appearance of being a machine himself, worked by an intellect not his own. Yet he was evidently working with a will.

I stepped forward and stood before him, having first made a sign to Jack.

"James Redpath," I said; "surely it must be James Redpath?"

He started, and looked at me with a surly scowl, but said nothing. The name (of course I used his real name) seemed to remind him of something, but there was no recognition in his eyes. "Don't you remember Bob Easterley?" I said. He looked at me and then his eyes wandered. There was a muddled, wicked look about him, such as you will sometimes see in the eyes of a very bad-tempered man when he is drunk. "Don't you remember Penruddock?" I said, again of course using the real name. He started again, and I thought he brightened, but it was a queer sort of brightening.

"Penruddock?" he said. "Penruddock and Bob Easterley: curse him and curse the little beggar!" And then he gave a nasty laugh. His voice was thick, like the voice of a man half stupefied with drink or suffering from active brain disease. I thought at first that the name Penruddock had awakened no recollection in his mind, but that he mistook it for the name of a man. Since then, however, I have thought that perhaps "the little beggar" was the boy that he was cruel to, and that the name of Penruddock had reminded him of the matter. Anyhow he turned and looked steadily at me and said slowly, "Oh, so the governor has got you; I wish you joy of the governor." And then he laughed a coarse, harsh kind of laugh. It was not loud, and there was not much expression in it, but what there was was cruel. Then he made as if to pass us, and we let him pass: there was nothing to be got out of him. I am not absolutely sure to this day whether he was James Redpath or not.

That night Jack and I talked long and earnestly. I told him as I have told you my latest thoughts about the matter, and then we talked of our engagements for the coming day.

Wilbraham. There's a crisis near, Bob. It is as likely to come to-morrow as not.

Easterley. How do you think it will come?

Wilbraham. Well, this way. Davelli, I think, overrates the power that he has contrived to get over you. The disappointment you speak of, and your distrust of him and resolve against him have somehow checked the effect of his action on your will, and he does not know that. Not knowing it, he will reveal some villainy to you to-morrow. You will revolt and he will try to kill you. If you are on your guard you may escape yet. The minute you defy him shoot him through the body.

Easterley. What harm will that do him?

Wilbraham. Not much, but some. Did you notice what he said yesterday?

Easterley. Yes, and he was telling the truth. The shot would probably send him to his own place, but he will be back again presently.

Wilbraham. Yes, but meanwhile you will have got a start, and if you are in one of the cars and can manage it you may escape.

Easterley. Not very likely; but supposing I did, what is to become of you?

Wilbraham. I shall be working for myself all the time. Look here: this fellow who is to guide me will either try to kill me or to put me in the way of killing myself. I believe that he has instructions to that effect. I'll watch him, and if I see any treachery I'll send him to his own place and make off if only I can manage the car. For I intend that he shall take me into one of the cars. Then I will try to join you and we shall have perhaps a start of an hour or so before they get back and make ready to follow us.

I didn't see much chance of success in his plan. You couldn't look at it anywhere, I thought, without finding a flaw in it, and I told him as much.

"Never mind," said he, "it is the unlikely thing that happens: let us be on the watch."

Easterley. On the watch, certainly; but look here, Jack: you and I are in imminent danger of death, but I am in danger of worse than death.

Wilbraham. Yesterday, perhaps; but not now, Bob.

Easterley. In one sense, more now than yesterday. I have given him power over me to-day; not so much perhaps as he thinks—you may be right there—but more than I may now be able to withstand. Besides, mark me, he is not going to bring things to a crisis yet.

Wilbraham. Well, if he is not, we shall bring things to a crisis ourselves, and we shall defy him. Then let him kill us if he can. I shouldn't wonder if he couldn't after all. Anyhow, I shall learn something to-morrow, and don't you put yourself in his power any more.

Easterley. I have told you that I am not sure if I can escape him now, but, God helping me, I will do my best.

There our talk ceased for the night, and I may as well say at once that the crisis did not come next day, and that it was not left either to Signor Davelli or to ourselves to bring it about. If it had been so left I do not think this book would ever have been written.

We were now sitting in the inner chamber, from one of the windows of which you could see the door of the outer chamber. The inner chamber opened into the outer, and the outer chamber, without any porch or passage, opened upon the path which led either to the square or the great stairway. As I sat near the window I saw a bright light shining upon the outer door, so that no one could go in or out without being plainly seen. I started up at once and looked for a shadow, for it occurred to me immediately that this light was thrown from one of the invisible cars. But there was no moonlight, for the moon was just then hidden by clouds, and so there was no shadow except such as the light itself might cause. But presently, by walking backward from the window and again towards it, and then this way and that way before it, I discovered a star which appeared and disappeared as I walked. On further inspection it became evident that when the star disappeared it was hidden by some object which, though dark itself, was nevertheless that from which the light before the door proceeded. There could be no doubt that the light in question was thrown from one of the cars, and that the car from which it was thrown was not a hundred feet from the ground.

"Look," I said, "look! we are closely watched even here." But Jack was already fast asleep. I threw myself upon my bed and lay for hours broad awake.

CHAPTER IX

THE SEED BEDS

As I lay awake the events of the last few days passed and repassed before my mind, and the more I thought over them the less I felt myself able to give any satisfactory account of them or to see any way of escape. I could make up my mind to no plan of action, to nothing except passive but obstinate resistance.

But although I did not see any way of escape I did not feel as if we were going to die. I suppose that youth and a sanguine temper enabled me to keep hoping. Anyhow I found myself again and again reckoning upon a return to civilisation.

But what kept my thoughts busiest was the fact that Jack and I were to be separated next day, and I asked myself over and over again, what could be the purpose of such separation. And here, after a while, I thought I saw my way a little. Such and such at least I felt I could say is not the purpose. Foul play is no doubt what our host is quite capable of; but what is to be gained by foul play? Why not kill either or both of us openly if he wishes? And when I had gotten as far as that I began to see, clearly enough, part at least of his purpose in separating us. And the revelation was greatly more flattering to Jack than to myself. Then I fell asleep and slept quite soundly for some hours, and I got up quite refreshed.

After we had dressed and refreshed ourselves there still remained an hour before it would be time to keep our appointments. For Jack had arranged with the man who had been told off to keep him company to meet him at nine o'clock, the same hour at which I was to meet Signor Davelli. And here I may as well mention that these men or whatever they were, understood our way of reckoning time. But they did not, as far as I could see, make use of it themselves. They had a method of reckoning time but I was not able to discover exactly what it was. I have sometimes thought since then that they were able to measure the earth's diurnal motion directly. But they used no clockwork nor (as far as I could see) any observation of the altitude of sun or stars.

In some of the cars which were fitted for long voyages there was fixed an instrument about a foot long, and this consisted of a hand moving along a graduated scale. I made sure (so far as my very brief opportunity of observation permitted) that this hand did not move by clockwork, but I was quite unable to discover by what power it did move.

I told Jack very briefly about the light I had seen last night, and then we held a brief conference before we parted.

"Jack," said I, "you thought yesterday that Signor Niccolo had given his man instructions either to kill you or to put you in the way of killing yourself?"

"Yes," he said, "under certain circumstances. If I attempt to make my escape the fellow is undoubtedly under orders to compass my death. But not otherwise; certainly not at present. And I need not say that I am not going to attempt my escape without you. If you and I agree to force a crisis, good and well; then we shall both run the risk of our lives. But you seem to think, and I am disposed to agree with you, that we had better for the present keep on the watch and let things take their course. Very well, then, I shall not be in any special danger to-morrow."

"Why do you think so?"

"Because, as I have said before, this man, or call him what you will, has got some design upon you. What that design is will probably appear shortly. And he will not hinder the success of it by allowing anything to happen to me."

"And if it succeeds?"

"Then it will depend on circumstances not now evident what will become of me."

"And if it fails?"

"Then I think that you and I are certain to be put to death unless we can manage to make our escape from this place."

"Which appears hardly to be expected."

"Yes, hardly to be expected, but the unexpected happens."

"And now, Jack," said I, "I agree with you in all that you have said; but do you know why he is sending you away?"

"Well, no, I don't."

"I'll tell you why: he fears your influence over me. I came to that conclusion as I lay awake last night. And he means to try on some new game to-day or to begin to try. But as I thought over all that I couldn't but go on to ask, why does he want me and not you, and why is he shy of you? What do you think?"

"I can't say, Bob, unless it be that I am not clever enough."

"Clever! you're a modest man, Jack, I know, but if I did not know you to be genuine I should say now that some of the modesty was put on. Not clever enough? You've seen through this fellow sooner and farther than I. You might better say too clever, but that is not it either."

"Well, what is it, then?"

"You are too good for him. You have too quick and clear a perception of what is right, and you are not ready enough to let the lust of knowledge blind your conscience. But, please God, this fellow will find that I am not after all quite the sort of man he takes me to be."

"My dear Bob, I am just as likely as you are to have dust thrown in the eyes of my conscience, only a different sort of dust. Your turn has come first, that is all. You'll baffle him and then my turn perhaps won't come at all. Let us both keep our eyes open to-day. If I can learn how to manage those cars of theirs, and if they give us half a chance, we will make a run for it."

"Do you forget the light last night?"

"I forget nothing, but we will give them the slip somehow."

"Well, perhaps we may, for one thing is clear to me, Jack: those fellows once they come among us have to work under the same conditions as we."

"Did not Dr. Leopold say something of that sort?"

"Yes, and he was right; all that we have seen proves it: everything that they do is done by some chemical or mechanical or other contrivance, they have to get round their work just as we have; they know more of nature than we do, and so they can do more. But if we knew as much we could do as much as they."

"Well, all that is so much in our favour."

We were now at the foot of the stairway, and it was within a few minutes of nine. So we shook hands and parted. Jack went up the stairway, and I made my way to the square.

I saw in the centre of the square a car somewhat smaller than that in which we had travelled previously, but, like it, visible throughout. It was just alighting as I came up. Signor Davelli was standing in the square, and the man in the car was the same whom he had assigned yesterday to Jack, and as he alighted he addressed him with a few words and signs as before, and the man went away towards the stairway.

Signor Niccolo turned to me, and, after the usual salutation, he said shortly but civilly, "I have had a car prepared like the other. As we use them ourselves, you might find them awkward and even dangerous. I have left the larger car for your friend."

"Thank you," I replied. "I daresay we shall both do very well."

I was glad to know that Jack would have the opportunity that he wished for, and I felt sure that he would make the most of it. I felt confident now that we were on the verge of a desperate effort for freedom. It was likely enough, indeed most likely, that the issue of such an effort would be immediately fatal to us, but, if not immediately fatal, then I thought that we might escape. Meanwhile I was determined to observe as closely as possible every person and thing that should come under my notice to-day.

There was no difference between this car and the other except in respect of size. This one was a shade smaller. Also this one was furnished with some instruments which I had not observed in the other. There were two good field-glasses and a very powerful microscope. There were also some instruments whose use I did not recognise, but they seemed to suggest spectrum analysis. In addition to these there were some glass instruments that looked like test tubes, and other chemical apparatus of apparently simple construction, but quite unfamiliar to me.

We got under way just as formerly, and we moved rapidly towards the western end of the valley. I reckon that it was two miles, or perhaps a little more, from the eastern to the western extremity. The valley was bounded all round by hills. But I seemed to see to-day more than ever before an air of artificial construction about these. From some points of view this disappeared altogether, while from other points the evidence of it was all but conclusive. I made sure sometimes that I could detect the junction of a great embankment with the hills on either side, but in each case after I had got another view I was not quite so sure. Just the same impression, as I have told you, was produced on me by the view of the hills when I first approached them from the east; but the appearance or impression of artificial construction was very much stronger now.

I had on this day a very full view of the arrangement of the valley from end to end. You remember the large square in which on the second day we had seen the men drilled, and in which on the day after we had witnessed our host's wonderful disappearance and reappearance. You remember also the broad walk which led from the eastern stairway to the square. Very well; at the further end of the square that walk was continued. It was the same breadth all the way through, and it was planted with trees and with flowering shrubs, mostly of a kind which I had never seen elsewhere. On each side of it narrower ways branched off, leading to houses of the same style as those in which Jack and I were lodged. There was an air of trimness and regularity about the whole but no beauty. I can imagine one looking at the scene and pronouncing it stiff and formal and nothing more. But as I looked I felt that if there was no beauty there was at least an eerie suggestiveness that took the place of beauty. Seen from above, as we saw, even trimness and regularity

82

have an odd look. But after all the trimness and regularity of the scene were its least remarkable characteristics. The frowning hills with rampart-like ridges between them that might be walls or that might be natural embankments; the silence broken only by the whirr of our motion through the air, for there was no bird in the valley from end to end, and indeed no living creature of any sort except its human (if they were human) inhabitants, and I think a few snakes; the uncouth aspect of the chimneyless and smokeless houses; the absence of every object that might remind one of the cares and pleasures of life: no garden, or orchard, or playground, no child or woman;—all this formed altogether a picture as unearthly and inhuman as the barren surface of the moon. The odd-looking trees and shrubs which, as I have told you, were planted along the roadway, made this worse and not better. Their approach to naturalness made the unnaturalness of all the rest only the more apparent. Besides, their very presence made you feel that it was not nature, as on the surface of the moon, which caused the silence and desolation, but some foul and maleficent influence which was external to nature. The broad walk and the rows of houses both ended abruptly, abutting upon a belt of timber artificially planted. The trees were like the blue gum, they were so close together that no passage between them was possible, and as far as I could judge the intervals from tree to tree were quite equal and regular. This plantation extended a good way up the cliff on both sides, and it was a hundred yards across, or more. Beyond it was a space of about twenty feet, and then another row of trees of quite a different kind, and like nothing that I had ever seen. But as far as I could guess from such a height the leaves were as thick as the gum leaves, but in other ways much larger. This row of trees was nearly of the same depth as the other, and extended like it high up on either side of the cliff. I have little doubt that all these trees were intended as a defence against the vapours which were generated by certain works which were carried on beyond, and of which I must now try to tell you what I saw.

From what I have said it will be clear to you that there was only one way from the eastern part of the valley to the western, and that was through the air. No one could pass through either belt of timber. And as we floated over them I noticed that Signor Niccolo at once raised the car several hundred feet, and kept well away to the south. Then he stopped; then he lowered the car a little and asked me what I saw.

I saw several very unequal belts of what seemed to be cultivated ground. But it was a very queer-looking sort of cultivation. There was almost no green from end to end of it, and what green there was looked like the scum that you sometimes see floating upon the surface of a stagnant pool. And even this was only to be seen at the southern extremity of the cultivated ground. As you looked north the growth was more and more foul and offensive, and thick, filthy looking vapours floated over it here and there. I thought of Shelley's ruined garden, where—

> "Agaric and fungi with mildew and mould
> Started like mist from the wet ground cold."

Only that here certainly it was not lack of care that produced all the foulness, for there was plenty of evidence of care everywhere. The beds were divided according to a well-marked plan: they were six in all. The bed on the southern extremity must have been over two hundred and fifty feet wide, and it had several narrow pathways through it, well formed from end to end. Then there was a wide pathway, say about eight feet in width, separating it from the next bed. The next bed was only half the width, with about half as many narrow pathways through it, and then a walk twice as wide as that which separated it from the first bed. Then the third bed was only half the width of the second, with a separating walk of about thirty-two feet across. And so on, the width of the beds decreasing and the width of the walks increasing in geometrical progression, so that the last bed was only about eight feet wide, while the walk beyond it was about two hundred and fifty feet wide.

All the beds and walks were the same length. As I was making these approximate measurements mentally, with the aid of a powerful field-glass, I observed another fact that seems worthy of notice. The foul growths and vapours which, as I have told you, increased from the southern extremity of the ground northward, came absolutely to an end with the last bed but one. But the last bed, which was the narrowest, with the walks on either side of it which were the widest, occupied more than a third of the whole extent of the cultivated ground. The true extent of the foul growths and vapours was about this: they covered rather more than a third of the ground, and the space which they covered was rather nearer the southern end than the northern end. I had reason to believe before the close of the day that these vapours were deadly; but I had reason also to believe that there was something in the bed to the north beyond them which was deadlier still.

There were many men employed at all the beds, much the greater number at the first bed, but the work at the sixth bed seemed to be far the more important; certainly it proceeded, as far as I was able to judge, with far more care and deliberation. Not, however, that there was anything slovenly about any of the work or of the workers.

I first turned my attention to the first bed, and there I saw a number of men at about equal distances on each of the walks, each provided with an instrument like an elaborate sort of hoe, and having a box slung round his shoulders, and hanging directly under his face. Looking along these rows of men to the far edge of the beds, I saw that the valley ended at the west end with a platform, and on this platform several men were standing who were evidently working in concert with the workers at the beds. This platform was not so high as that at the east end, but, unlike that, it extended the whole width of the valley. It consisted of two terraces connected by steps, and on the lower terrace were the men whom I have mentioned who were working in concert with the workers at the beds. One man stood at the end of each walk, and handed to the nearest man on the walk a parcel, and then another and another. He took these parcels out of a little box on wheels that stood beside him. These parcels were marked and numbered. At least so I concluded from the manner in which the man on the walk received each parcel, glanced at it, and passed it on. This distribution of the marked parcels had commenced before I began to observe.

Looking to the boxes on wheels, I saw that they were standing on rails, and were constructed so as to run on the same principle as the little waggons at the eastern end. Following with my glass the course of the rails on which they ran, I saw on the upper platform whither the rails led several machines in general appearance not unlike some of those at the other end. The glass which I was using was very powerful, much more powerful than any field-glass I had ever seen. Still, I could not observe with any such exactness as if I were standing by the machines. The car that I sat in, although there was not a breath of wind, was not absolutely still. I should not perhaps have noticed this if I had sat still and talked, or even read, but the moment I began to observe closely some object not on the car, I became conscious of a motion such as would be felt at sea on a calm day if there were a long but very gentle swell.

I saw with enough exactness, however, to conclude that the processes which were being carried on here were not mechanical, but most likely chemical. I could see many jars and retorts and instruments of similar aspect, and I thought I could make sure that electricity was being largely applied, and that some strange use was being made of light. It seemed as if there were some substances in certain small vessels on which now and then light greatly magnified was being thrown. These vessels were arranged in order within the machines in such way that they could be subjected at the will of the worker to the various light, magnifying, and chemical and electric processes which it seemed to be the function of the machine to keep in action.

I did not feel sure at first whether the substances in the vessels were being simply examined, or whether they were being treated with a view to effect some change in them. But I soon saw that the latter was the more likely purpose. For I perceived on further observation that they were subjected to a very severe and exact scrutiny before they were placed in the vessels. At one end of the row of machines was a very long table along which, near the middle, a trough ran from end to end. A man stood at the table who seemed to be examining something in the trough with a microscope, or at least with some sort of magnifying apparatus. Then he laid aside the magnifying apparatus, and poured from a little bottle either some fluid or powder, I could not tell which, on the objects which he was examining; then he would apply the magnifier again, and so on. Last of all, from this trough he would take up something or other with a little shovel or trowel, and place it in certain tiny waggons or boxes on wheels which communicated, apparently by automatic means such as I have before described, with the different machines, emptying their contents into the small vessels of which I have told you. All the machines appeared to be of the same sort, and engaged in the same work. I concluded that the man at the table with the trough in it was examining certain substances, and that these were being treated by the men at the machines with a view to some modification of their nature. And I had no doubt that this work, whatever it was, stood in some direct relation to the work at the seed beds.

If I had had any such doubt it would have been removed by what I observed at the other end of the row of machines. There I saw a table just like an enormous billiard table, only there were no pockets, and at this table stood four or five men busily at work. This table was connected with the seed beds by the rails, along which ran the boxes on wheels. Indeed, it was to it that my look had first been directed when I followed, with my glass, the course of these boxes. But the more curious aspect of the machines had attracted my attention, and I had observed the whole row of them to the other end and the table with the trough in it which stood there, before observing this end more particularly. I now saw that the substances which had been examined in the trough and treated in the machines were carried, still by automatic machinery, to this enormous table and emptied upon it. There they were very rapidly sorted and distributed into parcels by the five or six men at work there. These men must have had great accuracy of eye and touch, and their way of working reminded me of the man in the Mint who rings the coin. The parcels which were so made up were distributed among the workers in the seed beds in the way already described.

It was clear to me now that some substances, probably germs of one kind or another, were being examined and treated by scientific methods, and were being subjected afterwards to some sort of discriminating culture. I began to guess at the purpose of all this, and quite suddenly a suspicion broke upon me which almost made me drop my glass with horror. And I may as well say here at once that knowledge which I obtained later on confirmed this horrible suspicion.

Recovering myself, I turned my attention to the workers at the seed beds. The men engaged at the first bed went slowly along the walks taking every now and then something out of the boxes which were slung one over the shoulder of each, and planting it in the ground and covering it over. I saw that they examined also something already planted, and sometimes took it up and put it into the box. I could not tell, owing to the distance and the motion, whether or not what they took up exhibited any visible growth. The substances, whatever they were, which were thus taken up, were placed in a little waggon which ran at the eastern end of the bed at right angles to the walks, and conveyed its contents to the walks which separated the first bed from the second, and were dealt with by the workers there. If you ask me how I knew that it was the substances exhumed and not the substances in the parcels that were thus passed, I can only say that such was my conclusion from the whole aspect of the movement, for I could not accurately distinguish small objects at the distance.

The way of working at the next four beds was not so different from what I have described, as to make it worth while attempting a detailed account. It will suffice to say that the mode of procedure was to sow something in each bed, and to take up something which had been down in order to transfer it to the next bed, and this latter process evidently involved much careful examination and discrimination. I should also mention that at the third bed and onward the workers wore masks, apparently wire masks of some elaborate construction. They wore them, not continuously, but whenever they stooped to the ground or examined very closely the substances with which they were dealing. At other times the masks

87

hung at the girdles. At the fourth bed the workers wore the masks more frequently, and at the fifth they only removed them occasionally. The way of working at the sixth bed was different and will need a fuller description.

But before attempting to describe it I should say that just as I was beginning to observe the sixth bed, a slight change came in the weather which made two considerable changes, each in a different direction, in my opportunities of observation. It had been quite calm and at the same time cloudy. Now a light breeze began to blow and the sun shone out. The effect of the breeze was, at first, so to increase the motion of the car as to make very close observation impossible. But Signor Davelli presently applied a sort of ballasting machinery, which had the effect of greatly steadying the car. I was so much interested in what was going on below that I did not very accurately observe how this was done. But I think that it was somehow in this way. He moved, by mechanical contrivance, certain weights in the car, so as to change the centre of gravity in such manner as to render the part of it which we occupied subject to less motion than the rest. I have not much skill in such matters and I hardly know if this is possible, but so it seemed to me. But even after this was done the car was not by any means as steady as before.

At the same time, however, the sunshine which now appeared disclosed some features of the scene which I should otherwise have missed. For now, at the northern end of the beds, on a platform at right angles with the western platform, I saw several shadows which indicated to my now skilled eyesight the presence of several of the invisible cars. They were standing all still when I first saw them, but presently one moved, rose quickly from the earth, and passed gradually out of sight to the northward. I followed its course with my glass for several minutes, till it was nearly out of sight. I then turned again to the seed-beds. The men at the sixth bed were very few, only five in all, and each was working apparently on his own account. But they were all doing exactly the same kind of work. They were, as I thought, making a final selection of the germs which had undergone so careful a process of cultivation. Each of them had three boxes, instead of one, slung in front of him, and a long instrument in his hand with which he extracted certain substances from the ground. This instrument was constructed so as to hold in a little receptacle what was lifted from the ground. Each of the workers, also, had slung over his shoulder what looked like a small frame. I selected one of the five at random, and watched his proceedings more particularly. Now and then he would unsling the frame and place it on the ground. Then he would give it a little twist, whereupon it would assume a form very like that of a lady's work-table. I saw him do this many times, and each time he took something out of the closed receptacle which I have just mentioned, and placed it on the table, and observed it carefully with some kind of instrument that might have been a kind of microscope. After a more or less minute observation each time, he placed the substance observed in one of the boxes at his girdle, which he opened each time and carefully closed again. By-and-by he seemed to discover some substance which challenged his attention specially, for after a longer observation than usual, he took another instrument from his girdle and observed it more carefully and for a longer time. Then I could see that he called his neighbour, for he looked, and I almost thought that I could see his lips moving, and immediately the other looked up and came towards him. Then the first man handed his observing instrument to the second, who examined very carefully the substance on the little table. Some discussion seemed to follow, an animated conversation as I thought, with certainly a rapid pantomimic accompaniment.

Then a very strange thing happened. As the first man stooped towards the table his mask fell off. My glass was so good that I saw it quite plainly come loose at one side, and I saw the man's hand lifted up to catch it. But before he could reach it, it fell off as I have said. Then in a moment the man's body became a mass of rapidly seething fluid, and the fluid became a dark cloud of smoke, which spread into the air and disappeared. Just so I had seen Signor Davelli's body transformed and disappear the day before. The second man at once caught up the mask and stood apparently waiting. Presently a diffused vapour appeared. This became denser and denser, until it assumed the appearance of a seething fluid, as before. This quickly became consolidated and assumed the form of a body, the body of the man who had just disappeared. Then the other man, who was standing ready with the mask in his hand, fitted it again upon the first man, and both men proceeded to examine the substance before them, and to converse, as if nothing had happened to interrupt them. All this time (which, however, was a very short time, although the change was by no means instantaneous, as the like change seemed to be yesterday) the other men worked away without, as far as I could see, taking any notice whatever of what was going on.

I exclaimed slightly and started, and this attracted Signor Davelli's attention. He had been, I think, examining and preparing some instruments. "What do you see?" he said. I answered without taking my eyes from the glass. "A man over there disappeared and appeared again just as you did yesterday."

"Careless wretches!" he said, looking towards the place that I was observing.

"I suppose," I said, "that these substances which they are examining must be very deadly, for his mask fell off just before he disappeared, and I remember you said yesterday that what would kill us only drove you back into space."

"And you infer, I suppose, that if you had been in his place you would have dropped down dead."

"That is what I think," said I.

"Then you see if you become one of us you escape death." He said this with a strongly persuasive manner, and as he spoke a slight shudder seemed to pass over me, and I expected him to say more. But he said no more, and he returned to the task in which he had been engaged.

I then turned my attention again to my examination of the workers at the sixth bed.

You will understand that a very broad walk lay between the bed and the northern platform. This walk was to all appearance formed of some hard stuff like flags or asphalt, and I now perceived by the aid of the sunlight that some of the cars had alighted upon this pathway and were standing there.

I could see that there were five of them, and presently the five workers went over to the cars, one to each car. There was a man in each or beside each, I could not say which. For as you will remember I could only see the shadows of the cars, and the sun was now very high, and very near the zenith, and the shadows were proportionately small. The five workers took the boxes, each one from his girdle, one after another, and handed them, one after another, each worker to one of the men in or beside each car. Then the workers went back to the bed, and the cars rose from the ground. I could see that they rose almost perpendicularly at first for the shadows hardly moved, but became smaller and smaller; then they lengthened and passed away to the north-east, and rapidly disappeared. I looked up in the direction which seemed indicated by the lengthening shadows, and I could see distinctly for a few minutes something like a queer little cloud, and another and another until I counted the five. Then I lost sight of them.

If the north platform was the port of departure for the cars it seemed as if the south platform was the port of arrival. For now on looking straight below I saw that many cars were standing there, and some arrived as I looked. The bright sunshine enabled me to count them as they stood and to see them coming; and my position in respect of them enabled me to estimate the size of these cars by their shadows much more exactly than that of those which I had been just observing at the other end. A little further observation showed me that the cargo they were laden with consisted of the same sort of substances as those which were so carefully treated on the platform, and in the seed beds, and, finally, in a modified condition exported for use elsewhere. I had evidence already of the care which was given to the preparation and final distribution of these, and I now had evidence that the same kind of care was given to their first selection. Signor Davelli lowered the car to the platform, alighted, and called a man to his side. I alighted at the same time. The man came at once, and it was clear that he knew what he was called for; for he brought with him something that looked like a little glass case or tray, in which were a multitude of little matters which proved to be germs of some sort, part of them of animal and part of vegetable growth, and these, as I gathered, had been selected from a great number of similar matters which had just come in, and they were now submitted to Signor Davelli for his examination and approval. He examined them carefully in some ways that I understood, and in some ways also that I did not understand at all. As an instance of the latter I may mention the following. He extracted one of the germs from the case and placed it on an elliptical piece of opaque ware which was very slightly depressed in the middle. The germ was so small that he had to work with a magnifying-glass of enormous power, and with instruments of extreme delicacy. He showed me the germ through the glass. It was egg-shaped and colourless, with a tiny dark spot under a partly transparent substance. Without the glass it was to me absolutely invisible. Then he got a little glass tube into which he put something out of a very small bottle, which he took from a number of others which lay side by side in a little case which he took out of a pocket in the side of the car. Whether what he took out of the bottle was powder or fluid I could not tell, though I was now so near what I was observing. But I noticed that when poured into the tube it seemed to change colour. Then Signor Davelli handed the tube to the man who had come in answer to his call, and this man, who appeared to know exactly what was expected of him, took the tube and blew through it upon the germ. I could not see that anything came through the tube, but in a few seconds a kind of cream-coloured spray began to rise from the germ, and Signor Davelli observed this, not the germ but the spray, very carefully through the magnifier. He seemed highly pleased; he selected a few more germs

91

which he said were of the same sort as this; he spoke of them as particularly "promising," and he indicated, as I thought (for just here he began to speak in a tongue unknown to me), the treatment which in his judgment they ought to receive.

When I could no longer understand him I looked again to the workers at the beds. There were now a great many more workers at the first bed, and the work all through was proceeding in a very rapid and orderly manner. I followed quickly the whole process from first to last: the gathering in of the germs, their preliminary examination, the treatment which they underwent on the platform, the tests to which they were subjected before and after that treatment, their gradual passage through the several stages of cultivation, and finally their dispersion, in their cultivated condition, whither I could not certainly say, but presumably to the ends of the earth.

One thing especially puzzled me: I could not estimate at all the amount of time which the process of cultivation consumed in the case of each germ. There were germs constantly going into cultivation and frequently coming out; but how long it was from the time that each one went in until the same one came out again, whether they took different periods of time or uniform, or nearly uniform periods, I could not at all guess. The rapidly decreasing size of the beds implied certainly that the process of cultivation was a process of elimination. It seemed that not one in a hundred of those which passed through the first stage could ever have reached the final stage. And I think also that it might be inferred with much probability from the same fact that the process of cultivation lasted in most cases for a long time. For otherwise they might surely have made up for losses during culture by an increase of the numbers put under cultivation. For what I saw left me no room to doubt that such an increase in quantity was at their disposal. Making a rough estimate, I should say that hundreds of germs cultivated up to the highest pitch were sent away every day, and that hundreds of thousands went under cultivation.

While I was making these calculations, I became aware of a disturbance at the first bed. Turning my glass hastily to the spot I saw that one of the men had fallen down, and it struck me at first that there was going to be a repetition of the sort of disappearance and reappearance which I had already witnessed, and which I now understood. But I very soon saw that this was quite a different matter. There was a panic, and the men ran in all directions away from the man who had fallen. I followed for a moment with my glass the course of some of the fugitives. Turning the glass back towards the spot where the man had fallen, I could perceive nothing at all. Every trace of his body was lost. Then I heard a long and loud whistle, and in almost as little time as it takes me to tell it the panic had ceased and the men were working away just as before. Just then I heard what seemed like a deep and desperate curse from Signor Davelli, and looking towards him I saw him standing with his arm half way up, holding the glass. He seemed to have just taken it away from his eyes, and a scowl was passing over his face, made up as it seemed to me of malignity, ferocity, and fear. It reminded me at once of the expression which had passed over his countenance on the second day when the men were gathered in the square and when one or two of them proved to be missing, and I remembered also Jack's words, "Depend upon it his damnation has got something or other to do with the loss of these men."

To conceal my horror I turned my glass again to the workers, but I really observed nothing more, and presently at a signal from Signor Davelli I resumed my place in the car. He raised the car just as before, made a curve to the south, and then turned the prow of the car towards the east end of the valley. We alighted at the same point whence we had started, and then he spoke—

"Mr. Easterley, you know something of my power now."

I looked at him, I suppose, interrogatively, for he went on to say—

"Among your kings who is the most powerful? Is it not he who possesses the deadliest weapons and can use them with the most facility and precision?"

I said nothing for a moment, for I knew he was misleading me, or perhaps I should not say I knew, but I felt so, not indeed because of any opinion that I had formed about the purpose of the cultivated germs, but because of the profound distrust with which he had inspired me. Then, as he seemed to be waiting for my reply I said briefly, "I have no doubt at all of your power."

"Very well," he said; "we shall see to-morrow if you are worthy to share it."

I said nothing. The words that formed themselves in my mind were, "I hope that I am not sufficiently unworthy," but for obvious reasons I kept silence.

Then he said, "We meet here to-morrow two hours before noon, and now you can return to your friend; I can see him coming towards us on the stair."

I could not see, for I had left the glass in the car; but I exchanged a parting salute with my companion, walked slowly to

93

the stair and began to ascend it. Before beginning the ascent I had seen Jack standing half way up the stair, looking towards me.

After a hearty grip of the hand we turned back and walked slowly towards the pathway that we had taken on the second morning of our stay here. We spoke almost in whispers. I gave Jack a brief account of what I had seen. He said that it indicated something of which we could hardly guess the whole import, but he agreed with me that such import was probably as bad as it could be.

"We must try to escape," he said, "as soon as possible. I know now exactly how to work and steer the cars, and I know, too, how to lay my hands on a second battery."

"What do we want with a second battery?" said I.

"Well," said he, "I don't know what these batteries are made of; they are of solid stuff, not fluid, and yet they all waste very quickly. I doubt if any one of them will carry us as far as we may want to go; indeed, I am not sure that any two of them will be enough."

"But how are we to get away," said I; "we are so closely watched?"

"I'll tell you what I propose," he said. "We shall not retire to-night until an hour after dark, nor the next night, then we may hope that they will take it as a matter of course that we shall not retire on the third night until the same hour. But on the third night, immediately after dark, we shall make a bolt of it, and so we may hope for an hour's start."

"In the car?"

"Well, so I propose. I am aware that there is much to be said in favour of an attempt to escape on foot. These lozenges of theirs are meat and drink. We have had nothing else for several days, and we want nothing else, and we know now how many of them we should require, and it is certain that we could easily carry enough to last us three weeks or more. And if we make a bee-line for the wire we ought to reach it within three weeks or less. Besides, if we escape on foot they will not know where to look for us. We shall have cover among the trees, whereas in the air we shall have no cover."

"Not even if we escape in an invisible car?"

"There is none of the cars invisible to them."

"Ah! so I was beginning to think."

"I am quite sure of it."

"Well, go on."

"Still, three weeks may not be enough. We may not be able to make a bee-line. Probably we shall meet with some impassable scrub, or other obstacle, and so our food may run out, and we may

94

die miserably after all. But if we escape in one of the cars the whole risk will be over, and our fate will be decided one way or another within twenty-four hours."

"Very well," said I, "we shall try it the night after next."

Then I told him of my appointment next day with Signor Davelli.

He looked very grave. "That's the biggest risk of all," he said. "If you give in to him we're both done for."

"I won't give in to him."

"Good; but if he knows for certain that you are resisting him, he may take immediate action, and then also we shall be done for."

"He will give me more than one trial."

"I think he will, but, any way, we are not likely to have as much time as we thought. I would say, let us try to-night, but we are watched so closely, that it is not possible. We had better say to-morrow night."

"So be it," said I.

Then we went to our quarters and had some food and a little rest. Then we walked backward and forward on the same path again. About an hour after dark we retired for the night, and when we had passed into the inner room we could see the bright light already shining before the doors. The watch upon us was close and constant.

CHAPTER X

LEÄFAR

That night we lay both of us in the outer chamber, partly for company, and partly because neither of us wished to be within sight of the light which lay all night before the door, and which could be seen from the window of the inner chamber. There was nothing, indeed, strange or ugly about the light itself; it was very bright, and, under other circumstances, might have been pleasant. But to us, guessing whence it was and what was its purpose, it had come to have a weird look of doom about it.

We lay still, scarcely speaking. Only from time to time a word or two passed between us, either suggestive of preparation, or of some topic of encouragement. By and by we lapsed into silence, and thence into an imperfect sleep. There was no artificial light in our chamber, we had no occasion for any, although day and night were nearly of equal length. Sometime in the evening before dusk we used to take a second bath (if one may use the consuetudinal for so short a period), and then to throw off our hats and sandals and to exchange the long robe, which was our only other garment, for another of the same sort, was the whole of our preparation for the night.

I do not know how long I had been sleeping, but it could not have been very long, when I woke up with a start. Surely there was a light in the room? Yes, there was, and it was growing slowly brighter. I looked over to the couch where Jack lay; it was very near my own, but not near enough to permit me to touch him without rising.

I sat up and put on my sandals. The light had now become so much brighter that I could see Jack plainly. He was awake and watching as I was. The light was now increasing much more quickly, and in a few minutes the room was quite brilliantly illuminated, and there was a sort of core of brightness beginning to appear in the centre of the light. This presently assumed a wavering aspect, and by-and-by became a bubbling fluid. I was prepared to expect the appearance of a form of human similitude, for I had witnessed as you will remember, the same thing twice already. The same, and yet not the same, for the dark vapour which I had seen in the former cases was replaced in this case by a bright rose-coloured light. I suppose it was partly because of this obvious difference that I felt now no fear, but hope. I began to think that help was coming, and that we were not going to be left to fight out a desperate battle alone.

As I looked, the bubbling fluid became consolidated and assumed, as I had expected, a human form. A man of, it might be middle age, stood before us. I should have said much under middle age only that his expression indicated, as I thought, a ripeness of experience and a calm wisdom seldom seen in very young men. There was a stately beauty and benignity in his features and demeanour, a mingled tone of love and command and entreaty; all the direct reverse of what we had seen in Signor Davelli and his men. He wore a flowing robe of much the same pattern as ours, but it was of a very bright, indeed of a luminous material, and it had somehow a strange air of being part of his body. His head was uncovered; his hair was brown, short, and slightly curled, and his eyes were blue.

We both started to our feet, and made, almost involuntarily, a profound salutation.

"Friends," he said, "you are in urgent danger, and I come to inform and counsel and help you." He spoke the English language with a very sweet and firm intonation, and yet his accent was in some way suggestive of an outland or foreign origin. "I am a friend," he said, "and in some sort a guide of men. It was my mission long ages ago to warn your first father of the designs of an enemy of the same order as this one of yours, but far mightier than he. Later on in the plains of Assyria, under the name and form of a man, I baffled the designs of another of the same evil race. And many times in more modern days I have rendered help of which no record remains to man and to the friends of man. Speak to me freely; you may call me Leäfar."

I was meditating whether or not I should begin with a confession of my own faults, when Jack stepped forward, prevented me, and spoke.

"Sir Leäfar," he said, "tell us first of all who these men are into whose power we seem to have fallen, and from whom we desire to escape."

"Yes," answered he who called himself Leäfar, "it is best that you should have information first; counsel and help will follow.

"These men and I have one thing in common. We are inhabitants not of earth, but of ether; as they have themselves told you, we are dwellers in space. But they are not, as they would have you think, a fair sample of the race which inhabits the ether, for

97

although very many as compared with the inhabitants of earth, they are very few in comparison of those who hold with me."

"How is it possible," said I, "that you and they, although dwellers in space, or inhabitants of the ether, can assume as you do the form of men, and at least in some measure their nature?"

"I cannot," he replied, "unfold the matter to you in full detail, for you have not the faculties needful to enable you so to apprehend it; but if you will attend I will try to show you by analogies how it is possible for us to pass from our world to yours. But sit down," he said; "you will be weary, for I have much to say, and there is no time to lose."

Hereupon he sat down, having first indicated to us with a gracious air where we were to sit. We both sat in front of him, but each one a little to one side. Then he began. "The material," he said, "of your world and of such worlds as yours is limited. The material of our world envelops and pervades it all, and extends to immeasurable distances, as I believe to infinity, but the knowledge of infinity is reserved to the Infinite One Himself.

"The material of our world is the basis of the material of yours. The latter is made out of the former by a simple process of agglomeration. All the material of worlds like yours is resolvable ultimately into extremely minute particles, each of which is just a little twist of the ether. You may compare these particles to knots that you make upon a cord. Just as the parts of the cord in the knot act upon one another in a way in which they could not act if they remained in one continuous line, so the knotted or twisted ether becomes capable of a great variety of interactions which are not possible to it in its original state, and as the knots increase in complexity these possible interactions are multiplied. The motion by which the first agglomeration of ether is formed generates the various processes which are known to you as heat, magnetism, electricity, and the different chemical affinities, and so the matter of your world is built up. The bodies of the dwellers in ether are composed of ether in the simple state, and by a process which is simple enough although not fully explicable to you, we can transform them into the material of which your bodies are made and retransform them again.

"Two analogies, one mechanical and one chemical, may help you, if not to understand the process at least to see how it is possible. Suppose a string of immense length so thin as to be quite invisible; and suppose it to be knitted and woven and re-woven until it be formed into a piece of cloth, compact but very small. Suppose the process of knitting or weaving to be performed very quickly, and then suppose the web so formed to be as rapidly unravelled again. In that case the piece of cloth would appear and disappear just as you have seen our bodies do.

"Or suppose two vast masses of oxygen and hydrogen in the proportions in which they exist together as water. Suppose them to be brought together and subjected to the chemical process which is needed in order to make them combine: what happens? A small quantity of water suddenly appears. Reverse the process and it disappears.

"By means roughly analogous to these we are able to assume terrestrial bodies and to pass into the ether again. But while our bodies are in terrestrial form they are subject to the same laws as yours; we need food and sleep, and we are subject to the various accidents and conditions of humanity."

Here he paused for a moment and Jack spoke.

"But you are not subject to death as we are. Any cause that would kill us only resolves your material bodies into their ethereal form."

"That is the case," he said; "but the difference is not such as you suppose. All the material of your bodies is ultimately resolved into ethereal matter, but not all of it is essential to your being, and that which is essential is resolved by a much speedier process.

"But to speak of ourselves: while we remain in our own world we have instruments of sensation fitted to our condition and analogous to yours, just as hearing is analogous to seeing. But I cannot explain to you any more exactly our means of sensation, just as you could not explain sight to a man born blind.

"But our sensations are throughout strictly analogous to yours and pass into yours when we assume terrestrial bodies."

Here he paused again, and I asked, "Can you see our worlds from yours?"

"No," he replied. "The ether as far as we know pervades the universe and passes freely through worlds like yours, and we, while dwelling in the ether, have no more cognisance of your world than you of ours.

"But there are certain links," he added, "which bind both worlds together, and two of these are known to you as light and gravity. Our world is for ever in motion; motion is of the essence of its being, and it communicates its motion to all that is formed out of it and continued by it as your worlds are. Such motion is communicated in exact proportion to the vastly varied complexities of the matter of your worlds, and out of this proportionate communication arise the movements and the laws of movement of all the stars and planets, all of which movements and laws of movement are amenable to calculation. Much of this is already known to you, and the day will probably come when your men of science will be able to calculate the proper motion of the remotest star that your instruments can discover with as much precision as they now calculate the motions of your moon.

"Light is another link between your worlds and ours. And light is the one means which we have of detecting from our world the presence of yours. Not that we see light as you see it. The sort of perception that you have by means of light we have in our world by analogous but higher means. The presence of light is known to us when in our own world only by a slight shuddering motion of the ether. Just as you perceive a difference in the mode of motion when you travel on land and on the water or in the air; just so we perceive an analogous difference when we pass to the regions of light from the regions where light is not. A shuddering motion of the material of our world warns that we are where your worlds are. And just as for you sometimes the motion of the air or water passes into a hurricane or a whirlpool, so to us a vastly increased movement of the ether (not the regular movement which is the cause of gravity, but a quivering movement) indicates the presence of one of the secular outbursts of conflagration which form part of the process by which your worlds become fitted for your occupation."

"But how," inquired I, "can you come into our world without having any direct sensation of its whereabouts?"

"Once we have been here," he said, "it is a matter of easy calculation to us to fix the locality; and we can communicate the elements of the calculation to others who have not been here."

Here he paused, and rose to his feet, and as we were about to rise he signed to us to keep sitting.

"Now," he said, "hearken carefully while I tell you of those into whose power you are fallen." And as he spoke it seemed to me that his attention was directed more especially to myself.

He went on—"The Infinite One, ages before your worlds were formed, called the ethereal host into being. And at first they were like your brute creatures, only with vastly greater powers and intelligence; yet, like them, for their vast powers were not under the control of any will of their own, for there was no such thing then as will, except the will of the Infinite One.

"But it pleased the Infinite One at last to give His creatures will. That which is His own prerogative He communicated to them in order that He might give manifold scope to the eternal love which is His essence. That will of theirs it was His will that they should exercise in conformity with that eternal love. But being free it might oppose that eternal love, not indeed to eternity, but for incalculable cycles of time.

"A few, a very few, as compared to the whole number, opposed themselves to Him, and as the ages passed these grew ever more evil, and ever more full of hatred of Him and of all who hold with Him. A very few they were as compared with those who held with Him, but a great many when compared with all the men who inhabit this little world of yours, or who ever have inhabited it."

Here he paused again, and there was dead silence for a space, and then Jack spoke, and his voice was like that of a man hurried and somewhat overawed.

"But how did the will to resist the will of the Infinite One ever come into being at all?"

"It was a possibility from the moment when the first free being was created, and it became actual by the gradual and undue admixture of things in themselves good. The desire to do great things is good, and the joy to be able to do great things is good. But if these two good things are suffered to govern the whole being, they become the possible germs, inert as yet, of self-assertion and pride. And then when the call for self-sacrifice comes, as it must, to the finite in the presence of the Infinite, the will, the spark of divine life which the Creator has committed to the creature, rises up against the sacrifice, and by its action fertilises the germs of self-assertion and pride.

"So began the deadly war of the finite with the Infinite. That had its origin in 'worlds before the man,' and it speedily passed over into man's world, and would long ago have destroyed it had not the Infinite One Himself become human in order to teach men by His own example and in His own Person the divine lesson of self-sacrifice."

Here Leäfar paused again and sat down, and seemed to wait for some question from us. I was quite powerless to speak. I felt quite awe-stricken and shamed, but presently I heard Jack's voice ringing out clearly and confidently like the voice of a fearless and innocent child.

"Sir Leäfar," he said, "do the men who inhabit this valley belong to the evil race you speak of?"

"Yes," he replied, "they are some of the least powerful, though not the least evil among them."

"And what is their purpose here?"

"Their purpose in general is to set the inhabitants of your world against the will and purpose of the Infinite One, to teach them to call evil good and good evil. And they work out this purpose by a great variety of methods.

"They assume human forms, and they have dwellings in the most inaccessible parts of your worlds, near the summits of the loftiest mountain ranges, and in the polar regions, and in remote islands, and in deserts as here. When civilised men move into their neighbourhood they move away; and they destroy most of the marks of their occupation. Sometimes nothing remains; sometimes, it may be, a few huge rocks standing on end, or piled one upon another. Such remains, when you discover them, you account for by attributing their formation to races of men who have passed away.

"From these remote settlements of theirs they make excursions into the inhabited world; they mingle sometimes among men, stirring them to murder and rapine, sowing discontent among the people, and prompting rulers to tyrannous deeds of cruelty and violence. This Niccolo Davelli, as he calls himself, was very active in the most corrupt and violent years of the tenth century, when he was the active adviser of an Italian bandit baron.

"But they have seldom taken prominent action in their own persons in more modern times, although here and there they appear in subordinate characters, stirring up strife and all kinds of evil, and then they pass elsewhither.

"But this Davelli has lately taken up a line of action against God and man which some of the more powerful of his kind took up ages ago with far wider success; he has established here, and in the inaccessible parts of the Himalayas, and in one or two other places, artificial seed-beds of pestilence. His emissaries gather, from all quarters, germs of natural and healthful growth, and submit them to a special cultivation under which they become obnoxious and hurtful to human nature. And then they sow them here and there in the most likely places, and thus produce disease, death, and disaster among men. The black death, and the plague, and smallpox, and cholera, and typhus and typhoid fevers have all had their origin in this way, and some of these are kept alive since by the carelessness of men. But of later years men are beginning to understand health and disease better, and so the power of these evil beings is becoming greatly restricted in this direction."

Here he paused again, and I took heart and said—

"Is it simply to gratify their love of inflicting pain that they cultivate and propagate these plagues?"

"Partly that, no doubt," he said, "but, above all, their purpose is to set men against the Infinite One by making them believe Him to be the Creator of painful and abominable diseases."

"But why should they not blame Him," said I, "if He has called into existence those evil beings who invent such diseases?"

"Suppose," replied Leäfar, "that a human enemy were to poison your water supply. Would you blame God or man?"

"Man, I suppose," replied I.

"Yes," he said, "for you would recognise the fact that man, being man, is free, and that once his freedom absolutely ceases he is no longer man. The Infinite One may, if He so please, take away his freedom, but by so doing He annihilates the man."

"You raise a hard question," said I; "is the Infinite One, then, committed to the eternal prevalence of evil? Is He pledged never to annihilate the power to do evil?"

Leäfar answered very slowly and solemnly, and yet there was a smile upon his countenance as he spoke.

"There is one thing impossible to the Eternal Love, and that is to annihilate Himself: and it would be to annihilate Himself if He were to permit the existence of Eternal hatred."

"Then," said I, "if I understand you rightly, these beings are doomed to annihilation?"

He smiled again and said, "Surely the freedom which opposes and continues to oppose God must perish: it is self-doomed; that is as certain as that the Love of God is infinite. The creature who so misuses his freedom must lose it at last, and then he is as if he had never possessed it. And so his moral being is, as you say, annihilated. All his other powers remain, but his will is dead. He becomes, like the brute, or like the earliest of the ethereal creation; nothing but an instrument in the hand of God. Such is the eternal doom of those who choose evil and abide by their choice. No pain remains, no hatred remains, no sin remains, because no opposition to God remains. But no real soul remains. The moral being is dead and done with, only an intellectual being remains."

"And what becomes of them?"

"They become the beasts of burden of the universe: they become instruments for carrying on the various mechanisms of the visible creation. They become subject to us just as your horse is to you. Many such are under my own direction and control."

Here Jack started and almost interrupted him, then hesitated and said, "I beg your pardon."

"Say on," replied Leäfar, quite softly and kindly.

"What I was going to say," said Jack, "was this: It seems to me that the final doom of which you tell us must have come to some of them before this."

"Some of them are meeting it every day," said he. "The

103

mightiest of them can hold out for periods of secular vastness without losing their power of will in any appreciable degree; others, again, lose it all after a period comparable with the life of a man."

"And do they all know that they must lose it?"

"As well as you know that you must die."

"Ah!" said Jack, "I thought so, and now, sir, tell me one thing more: if this doom comes upon them while they are in human form, what happens then?"

"They pass back at once into their own world and are dealt with as I have told you there."

"Yes, I see it now. Two of the men here appeared to be missing the other morning, and when Davelli missed them I saw his face change with terror and malignity. I said to my friend here, 'Depend upon it the loss of these men has got something to do with his damnation.' Did I not say so, Bob?"

I nodded assent.

"It is true," said Leäfar.

"Then surely," said I, "they must be dying out rapidly."

"Dying out, certainly, but not as rapidly as you might suppose."

"Have they," said I, "the power to reproduce their kind?"

"No," said he; "the dwellers in the ether 'neither marry nor are given in marriage.' But they recruit their failing ranks from amongst men and from races analogous to man in other worlds like yours; they win them over to their side here and then claim them when they pass over there. Sometimes they steal them away from this world. Their purpose is to steal you away, one of you or both."

"Steal us! Surely that would not be permitted?"

"It is not possible unless you yourselves give yourselves away."

"How should we give ourselves away?"

"If you submit your will to theirs they get power over you, power which is hard to shake off, and which is very easily increased."

Here he paused, and the smile which usually attended his pauses did not appear. A sad expression, severe yet very gentle, took its place. There was a silence of several seconds. Then I stood up and spoke, standing.

"Hear me, sir. I remember and repent my faults. I knew that this man was a bad man. Nay, I had begun to suspect that he was something other and worse than a bad man. But I saw that he knew things which I longed to know, and so I suffered myself to forget his badness and I did for the moment submit myself to his will. He exercised his power upon me and he deceived me in its exercise. He

104

transferred me to the surface of the moon, or showed it me in a trance, I know not which. I am conscious ever since of being somehow in bondage to him; although I am now determined to resist him to the death. Is there any hope?"

"Yes, there is hope, surely, although you may have, as you say, to resist him to the death. But if you die resisting him he will have no power over you after death. I am come to rescue both you and your friend. He runs no such risk as you do, although you are both in great danger of your lives."

"And but for my compliance, I suppose neither of us would have run any risk at all."

"Not so. You were both of you in great danger of your lives, and your friend is still so. But any further compliance on your part will make you the slave of this man, living or dead."

I shuddered and said, "What is to be done?"

"Your penitence and your present purpose are accepted, and you will have one more opportunity of asserting your own will against this Davelli. Tell me what has passed between you since your first compliance."

I told him in brief all that I have told you in the last chapter.

"It is clear," said Leäfar, "that he is going to make one more attempt upon you. He will make it, no doubt, when you meet him to-morrow. If you surrender your will to him again I see no hope. If you resist, then he will have no power but over your body."

"And what will he do then?"

"I cannot certainly say. He may kill you in his unrestrained fury. It is not altogether unlikely that he will. But that is all that he can do. You will have escaped him, and I will be able most probably to extricate your friend. But I think it more probable that he will resolve to make one other effort to enslave you, and, in that case, before the effort is made, I shall probably be able to extricate you both. I have little or no doubt that I shall be able, although the strife will be hard."

It occurred to me to ask him why he would not rescue us at once, without waiting for any further conference between Davelli and me. But I knew what the answer would be, and I felt its force. I knew that I should be fit for nothing in earth or heaven until I had asserted my will against this evil being, so I answered simply, "How shall I resist him?"

"He will probably endeavour to throw you into a trance again, and if you give your will to him for a moment, he will succeed. But if you hold your soul firmly, then he will fail. Call inwardly upon God and give yourself to God with your whole purpose. Think all the

105

time of the holiest event in the history of mankind when the power of evil flung its whole force against One that was human, and was baffled, and the victory was won through suffering. So you will keep your will unsurrendered, and your adversary will be beaten back."

"And then?"

"Then, as I have said, he may kill your body in his disappointment and humiliation and rage, but you will be safe from him all the same."

"Let me escape him, and I am willing to die."

"That is the true temper; keep to that, and you need have no fear. And now listen to my further counsel."

But here again Jack interrupted him. "Surely, sir," he said, "it is better, is it not, to act at once? Why expose my friend here to a fearful risk? Lead us now, and we will follow you any whither. Let the risk, then, be what it may be, it cannot be more than the risk of death."

"Sir," said Leäfar, "I deeply honour your spirit and feeling, but you do not know the nature of the case. It is true that I might be able to rescue both of you from the place without any further contact between your friend and him whom you call Niccolo Davelli. I might be able and yet I might not, for although I am stronger than these men they have great odds against me here. But that is not the question, for suppose that I were quite certain that I could take you both alive out of this place, your friend remaining as he now is, I should not try to do so, for his own sake I would not. Wherever he would be, the power which this evil being has gained over him would remain and might be exercised at the most inopportune time for him. Davelli would select his own time, and that would be, no doubt, when your friend would be not so likely as now to resist him successfully. I see that you are willing to risk your life on his account, and your willingness will, no doubt, help him greatly. But not even all the wealth of sacrifice can save a man against his will. You may win his will but you cannot dispense with its exercise as long as he is man, or no less than man. Believe me that the very best thing that can be done for your friend is to let him take at once the opportunity which presents itself of asserting his will against the will of this evil one. He never can be more favourably disposed to do so than he is now."

It seemed as if Jack was going to answer, and I tried to catch his eye to dissuade him, for I felt very certain that what Leäfar said was true. But I could not catch his eye, and he tried to speak, but hesitated before a word came. Leäfar waited courteously. Jack made a further attempt. "But, sir," he began, and then again hesitated. At

106

last he said, "No doubt, sir, you know best; let me not interrupt you further."

Then Leäfar continued, addressing himself to me. "I will suppose, now, that you have been successful in your endeavour to resist your enemy, and that he has resolved to make one other attempt to subdue your will. For certain reasons, of which I am well aware, but which I have now no time to explain, I know that in that case another night will have to pass before the next attempt is made. And during that night you must make your endeavour to escape. Come back at once when Davelli leaves you and meet your friend at or near the entrance to these rooms. Go and take some rest and refreshment, for you will need them, and provide yourselves with as much food as you can carry with ease. Then wander whither you will, only not far, and keep well within the bounds of the valley. Make no attempt whatsoever at concealment while the daylight lasts. As the darkness comes on return hitherward and rest awhile within sight of these chambers.

"Wait there until you see two men about your own size enter the room, and until you see the light settle down as usual before the door. Then go both of you to the car"—(here he addressed himself especially to Jack)—"the car, I mean, in which you rode yesterday; start at once; lose no time, there is none to lose, for if you are pursued at all, you will be pursued before daylight. I will see that the car is well stored with food and provided with a spare battery and with glasses and light."

Here he added some further instructions, which I lost. Then I heard him say further,

"If you are followed I will follow, and I will help you as far as I may. There is everything to hope, and by that time there will be but little to fear. Barring unforeseen accidents you will escape with your lives. A brave man does all he can to save his life, but he is not afraid to lose it.

"Be sure, at any rate, that one good result will come of your adventure. These men will desert this place. No white man before you ever set his foot here, and these beings always conceal their earthly dwelling-places from civilised men. The next pioneers will find nothing here but, perhaps, a few odd-looking rocks.

"You may not need my assistance any more, but if your enemies follow you look up for a white flag and you will see that you are not alone."

Here he ceased and stood up, and we also stood up and bent our heads. He lifted his hand simply, and said "God keep you."

107

Then he disappeared in the same way in which he had appeared, but much more quickly.

It was still quite dark in our quarters although the day may have been beginning to break, and after exchanging a few hopeful words we tried to sleep. Strange to say I slept soundly, and I did not awake until it was full daylight.

When the appointed hour came I wrung Jack's hand in silence, and went to meet Signor Davelli. I reached the place of meeting only a few minutes too soon, and presently I saw him coming.

I knew that this was the hour of destiny for me, and I remember thinking that a man does not always know the hour of destiny when it comes, and that it would be better for him if he did. Then, of a sudden, it struck me that such reflection indicated a coolness that was hardly native to me, and, was it a good sign or a bad? I thought it was good, and yet that it was overdone. And I remembered to have read, "Let him that thinketh he standeth take heed lest he fall."

Just then Davelli came up, and I silently committed myself to God and awaited his onset. It came without any delay, but without any demonstration. He wasted no time, and he was evidently very confident. I was standing when he arrived, and after the usual exchange of salutations he invited me to sit down. I did so, and he sat down too, not beside me but opposite me. Then, almost immediately, he rose up again and looked straight into my face; rather, I should say, straight into my eyes. Should I look away from him? No; straight back into his eyes, and let him do his best. Then, as our eyes met, there began for me a series of desperate encounters of which there was absolutely no outward sign.

First, it seemed as if I were enduring the most imperious cravings of appetite—appetite as relentless and cruel as that which drove the Samaritan mother to devour her son; such appetite as has ever been ready to trample upon honour and hope and shame and love, for the sake of its own immediate gratification. Such keen, hungry sense of desire goaded me now, and along with its urgency came the consciousness, full, clear, and strong, that it would be gratified at once, if I would simply change the look of resistance with which I was meeting my enemy's eye for a look of acquiescence.

I do not know how long this lasted, it could hardly have been an hour, but it seemed like days and years to me. But at last there was a change, and of a sudden I became conscious of pain—physical pain multiplied and intensified indefinitely beyond all my experience or imagination—

108

> "All fiery pangs on battle-fields
> On fever beds where sick men toss."

All these seemed to wring me, and rack me, and strive to wrench the soul out of me, and ever as the pain grew, there grew also the consciousness that if I would but meet my enemy's eye with one moment's glance of acquiescence all the pain would be exchanged for ease; and oh! how delicious the very thought of ease appeared to be, more delicious than all the delights of all the senses.

Meantime, I was conscious of nothing external except the eyes of my adversary, the expression of which was an extraordinary mixture of persuasiveness and deadly determination, now and then crossed, however, by a furious flash of malignity, and again by a flash of hideous and awful terror.

But all the time also I was doing with all my might what Leäfar had bade me do, and it seemed to me as if my will were growing one with God's will, and it seemed to me as if I stood under the cross, and felt in my own flesh and sinews the very nails and thorns which pierced the Divine Sufferer.

Again there was a change; all at once there began to crowd into my mind in rapid succession all the questionings of life and of thought, of knowing and of being, that ever have tantalized the mind of man. And it seemed to me that only a thin veil was lying between me and the answers to them all. It seemed to me that the key of all knowledge was lying within my reach; as if the solution of all the moral and intellectual riddles that ever have plagued humanity were there now ready to my hand; as if all mysteries might be unsealed for me in one way, and only one way, and as if that way once again were to change my attitude of resistance, if only for a moment, for an attitude of acquiescence.

And now the burning lust of knowledge seemed to grow into a force, far exceeding all the other forces that had been brought to bear upon me. Rather it seemed to draw them all up into itself, and then to let them loose upon me. And for one dreadful moment I felt as if I must surrender. But with a sheer and last effort I offered myself to God.

And then a whisper seemed to speak within, and say that the solution of all mysteries was only to be found in the Divine Self-Sacrifice. And then it seemed as if the cross and the figure upon the cross filled all my sight, and the evil glare of the eyes that had been fixed upon me slowly passed away.

I don't know if I fainted, I suppose I did, but if I did I was roused by a loud and furious curse, and starting into consciousness

I saw Signor Niccolo looking at me with a look of baffled malignity, hatred, and fear.

"Wretch!" he said, "you have resisted me and you must die. And yet not now, nor easily. Go back to prison. To-morrow you shall suffer again all and more than all that you have suffered to-day. You are in my power beyond hope of escape; you must yield to me or die."

Then he put a little phial to his mouth, and his body seemed first to melt and then to boil, and then to pass into a dark vapour, and then to disappear almost as quickly as I have written the words.

After a few minutes I rose to my feet, saying, Thank God! I found that I was quite exhausted and scarce able for any exertion. I walked very slowly away.

I soon saw Jack standing near the foot of the eastern stairway. I made a signal to him and he hurried towards me. We met in a few minutes more; and in answer to Jack's look of anxious inquiry, I whispered, "I have beaten him," and Jack said, "Thank God!" and strange as it may seem, not another word on that part of the subject passed between us for months after.

We returned to our quarters and rested and refreshed ourselves, and then we compared notes briefly. We knew exactly what we had to do, and the time was at hand. About an hour before sunset we left our quarters for the last time, and wandered about without any attempt at concealment, and exchanging only a brief word or two now and then.

The night came on cloudy and dark, and still we stayed without. It was about an hour after dark when we saw such a light as that which rested every night before our door moving about hither and thither. It seemed as if the bearers of the light were in search of us, and we were beginning to wonder how best we should baffle their scrutiny. Just then we saw the figures of two men walk up to the door of our quarters and enter. Then the door was closed, and the light settled down before the door and all was quiet.

CHAPTER XI

ESCAPE

When we saw the light settle down before the door it was about eight o'clock, a little more than two hours after sunset. It was very cloudy but not absolutely dark. We turned our steps at once toward the stair. We had no expectation of any difficulty just yet. The watch which was kept upon us during the night was effectually neutralised; for the watchers, no doubt, supposed that we were safely housed, and that we could not stir without betraying our movements to them. Nevertheless, we walked very softly and spoke almost nothing until we reached the summit of the stair. Then we stopped and held a very brief conference. There were various points of detail as to which it was needful that we should understand one another more perfectly. But after glancing at them it seemed better that we should make a start first, and then we could converse without losing time.

So we hurried along the platform to the car. It was on the very spot where we saw it first, on the evening when we made our first voyage in it. Everything was ready. One battery was in position, and another lay by it ready to take its place. There was a pocket on one side of the car filled with the lozenge-like articles of diet on which we had lived since we came here. There were two glasses like that with which I had observed the seed-beds, and Jack, after examination, pronounced that there was an abundant store of the matters required for the production of the gas which was needed for the inflation of the balloons. The light by which we saw all this stood in the fore part of the car just over a little binnacle where a compass was fixed. Leäfar had more than fulfilled his promise.

I had noticed before in the cars a framework like this in which the compass was housed, but it never struck me what it was for. The compass card was very like ours. It had sixteen points only instead of thirty-two, and these were distinguished by colours and combinations of colours. The light was no doubt electric, for it was to all appearance produced by a battery acting on a system of wires. The wire did not seem to consume very rapidly, and it was supplied by automatic machinery from a large coil fixed under the binnacle. I have said "no doubt electric." I ought to add that the machinery which produced the light had no perceptible effect on the car's compasses nor yet on mine.

As soon as we got into the car Jack proceeded to raise it, as Niccolo Davelli had done, by inflating the balloons. This cannot be quickly done by any but a practised hand. If one who has had no practice tries it, the balloons are apt to get unequally inflated, and so the operator in bringing them every now and then to a state of equal inflation works the car from side to side with a rolling motion. Signor Davelli raised it quickly, without any rolling motion at all. This was only the second day of practice for Jack, but he managed by raising the car slowly to produce very little of the rolling motion.

As soon as he had attained what he judged a sufficient height he connected the batteries with the paddles, and as the wind was, as the sailors say, "dead aft," we soon began to make very great speed.

I noticed now a point in the machinery which I had not observed before. There was a valve to each balloon, and both valves were worked by a sort of movable tap, one tap for both. The effect of these valves appeared to be the maintenance of the cars at a uniform height, or higher or lower as the driver wished. The tap was worked by the same machinery that drove the paddles. And if the driver for any reason wished to make the balloon act independently of the paddles he could disconnect the tap which worked the valves from the machinery which worked the paddles. The connection and disconnection was made by a handle within easy reach of the driver.

After we had got well under way Jack began to speak.

"Now, Bob," he said, "do you think that you can steer while I speak? I have something to say. Here is the handle that you steer by: you see it is fixed so that you pull the way you want to go. That bright blue mark on the compass is East. Never mind the balloons, I will attend to them if there is need. You will have nothing to do but just keep the head of the car due east."

I found but little difficulty in managing the car as he directed, and after about twenty minutes' practice I was able to steer and listen at the same time.

Then Jack began, in a business-like manner, "You have seen the battery that we are driving by now; very well, here is the spare battery which, according to Leäfar's promise, I find." He pointed to the spare battery, which was placed on a sort of bracket within my sight. He took it off, or rather out of, the bracket with his two hands and put it back again.

"I see," said I, "that it is larger; it seems heavier than the other, and in some details different: what of that?"

112

"Thereby hangs a tale," he said. "I have not been able to learn anything about the way of making these batteries. Indeed, I did not try; there was no time to spare from the more urgent matters. What I have learned is that they have two kinds of battery, one much more easily made and which wastes very much more quickly, but which drives the cars faster while it lasts. That is the sort that we are using now. The other sort is more difficult of production and wastes very much more slowly, and drives the cars more slowly. On long voyages, as I understand, they use the latter sort mainly, reserving the former sort for short voyages and for spurts. Now the spare battery is of the sort that wastes more slowly and drives the car more slowly; whereas it is a battery of the other sort that has been put into operation, what does that mean? I don't know how Leäfar got the batteries, and I don't know what he knows about their use. I think it would not be safe to assume that he is beyond the risk of making mistakes. They have to learn things just as we have."

"He got the battery for us," I replied, "and it seems the safer thing to conclude that he knows more about it than we do. But what does it matter any way?"

"I'll tell you as near as I can. Don't mind a bit of rigmarole or what seems to be such. Trust me for coming to the point all the time."

"Go ahead," said I.

"Very well," he said, "I want to know, or to make as near a guess as possible, at two or three things.

"(.) How fast are we going now, and how far are we from the wire? or how far were we when we started? That means, how soon shall we reach the wire?

"(.) What are we to do if we overshoot the wire? We have no way of telling the longitude; my watch indeed is a capital chronometer, but I have altered it by the sun two or three times as near as I could. Besides, we cannot get the sun's place near enough. Now, if we overshoot the wire, we shall either have to cross the continent or else to make southward and look out for the Darling or for the Murray; or, failing either, for the sea.

"I do not think that we can have made much more than three hundred miles of westing from the Daly Waters, and suppose that we are now travelling at the rate of thirty miles an hour, which is not unlikely, we ought, if we keep up the rate, to make the wire at seven or eight o'clock in the morning. If I have overrated the distance or underrated our speed only a little, we may cross the wire before sunrise.

113

"So far, then, it seems clear to me that we ought to be travelling at the slow rate instead of the quick rate. I thought of this before, but I saw no means of securing one of the larger batteries, and I knew that I could slow the speed of the smaller one.

"Why don't I slow it now? you will say. Well, because I found the smaller and quicker battery put on, although the other was there: why was it put on unless to use all possible speed? I cannot but think that Leäfar considers the prospect of pursuit so great that speed is in his view the first necessity. I may be wrong, but, somehow, this view of the case makes me unwilling to slow the machinery."

"I think you are right," I said; "still it is quite possible that there may be nothing in it. The workers whom Leäfar employs may have been simply bidden to secure the batteries, and to put one of them on; the difference between the batteries may have been altogether overlooked."

"It may be so," he said, "and one must not overlook the possibility, but I don't think it likely."

"Then you see something in the presence of the larger battery?"

"That's it," he said. "If only the voyage to the wire were in view a second one of the smaller batteries would have given us an ample margin for contingencies. I think that the chance of our overshooting the wire has been reckoned upon, and for that reason the other battery has been provided. The smaller battery wastes in less than twenty-four hours, the other lasts, I believe, about four weeks. But the speed of the larger is not much more than half the speed of the smaller. Now, if we do overshoot the wire, a spare battery of the smaller kind would fail us in the midst of the bush, while the larger one would enable us to reach some settlement.

"Just one word more. We are now at full speed, and I found the machinery fixed for full speed when we came on board. Besides, the wind has not in any way changed since the middle of the day, and it is full in our favour now. Our speed is at the very highest, and whosoever put in the battery must have known that it would be so; even if the wind were to fall the difference would not be very great. Now, what do you say?"

Easterley. I think we must go as we are going until dawn of day anyway. If we are not pursued before then, we shall not be pursued at all.

Wilbraham. Why do you think that?

Easterley. It seems to be the way of these fellows to keep as clear of civilised men as is consistent with the pursuit of their malevolent purposes.

114

Wilbraham. What do you suppose to be their motive?

Easterley. Well, it doesn't seem very far to seek. Among civilised men there is very little belief in the existence of such beings; what little there is is usually not active, and so far as it is active it attributes to them, just as the belief of savage men does, powers greatly in excess of those which they really possess. Either state of mind is highly favourable to their ends, and anything substituted for either; a state of mind like neither would of course be avoided by them. They might almost live among savages without in any way detracting from a highly exaggerated view of their powers; but any decisive appearance of them among civilised men; any experience such as we have had, if established and accepted, would cause their powers to be examined and understood.

Wilbraham. I see; we should take their measure and know how to manage them.

Easterley. That's it; as Mr. Morley says of the clergy, we should explain them.

Wilbraham. And that would be worse for them than a sheer denial of their existence?

Easterley. Very much worse. Their motives and purposes would be known and canvassed like other matters of fact, and much that holds up its head in the world now would be discredited in consequence.

Wilbraham. In short, we may put our confidence in Leäfar's opinion, and we may conclude that they will not pursue us into the civilised settlements.

Easterley. I think so, and therefore my opinion is that when daylight comes if we find no trace of pursuit we may slack speed, and lower the car and look for the wire.

Wilbraham. Agreed. And now what do you think? Shall we be followed?

Easterley. On the whole I think we shall, but it depends on circumstances that we can only guess at.

Wilbraham. Why do you think we shall be followed?

Easterley. Well, it seems to me likely that patrols of some kind are kept, and in that case the absence of the car will be discovered, perhaps is now discovered.

Wilbraham. And what then?

Easterley. Then our quarters will be searched, and our escape will immediately become known.

Wilbraham. How can they tell in which direction to follow us?

Easterley. They cannot tell, but they may very well conclude that we shall make either for the west coast or for the wire, and they may send after us both ways. I wonder if Leäfar knows which course we have taken?

Wilbraham. Yes, he knows. I thought you were not attending when I said it, but I spoke plainly enough. I said, "If we escape shall we go eastward or westward? My purpose is to make for the wire." And he said in reply "Yes, that is the better course." It was near the end of his talk.

"Well, now," said I, "suppose we get through safely, what shall we do with the car?"

"I have thought that over, Bob," he said, "and I have come to rather an odd conclusion."

Easterley. Do you mind telling a fellow what it is?

Wilbraham. Not at all. Suppose now that we should steer this car to Melbourne or to Sydney and exhibit it. We should make a great noise, no doubt, and perhaps a pot of money, but we should ruin ourselves for all that. Even if we go to work like gentlemen, even if we make no attempt to make money out of it, but simply hand over the car to some public body with any statement we like to make, we shall be ruined all the same.

Easterley. I dare say you are right.

Wilbraham. Yes, I am right. For in the first place suppose we make a true statement, and neither of us would consent to do else, what will follow? Either we shall be set down as impostors without any more ado, or else an expedition will be organized to examine the country we have been in. But if Leäfar is right, as no doubt he is, nothing will be found to justify our story. Suppose we warn them beforehand that they will find nothing, that will be accepted as only one proof more that we are lying.

Suppose, now, for the sake of argument, that we do lie, and say that we ourselves invented and constructed the car, then we shall be expected and invited to make another. But we know next to nothing about the manner of producing the gas which inflates the balloons or about the constitution of the batteries. If we should attempt to substitute larger balloons filled with hydrogen, and batteries of such construction as we understand, the almost certain result would be that our car would be added to the long list of discredited flying machines, and ourselves to the much longer list of exposed impostors. How do you like the prospect?

Easterley. Not at all; and I believe you are right. But what do you propose to do?

Wilbraham. If we discover the wire I propose to go back two or three miles and abandon the car. I should like to break it up but we have no tools. I can dismantle it, however, so that nobody will be able to make anything of it if it is found.

Easterley. But if we escape we must give some account of our escape; we are not going to tell lies.

Wilbraham. Not lies; we shall tell the whole truth about the blacks, and for the rest we shall confine ourselves to generalities which will be true as far as they go. They may think us a little bit off our heads, "a shingle short," as Tim Blundell would say, but that won't matter, it will be set down to our wanderings in the bush. For the present at least we had better keep the whole matter as quiet as we can. If we ever see a chance of doing any good by speaking out we shall speak out. But now to more immediate business. Can we try to estimate the rate at which we are travelling?

By this time it was much brighter, the clouds were quite cleared away, and the moon, which was only two or three days past the full, was fairly well up in the sky.

So I said to Jack, "Lower the car a little, then take the steering gear in hand and let me try to estimate our speed." He let the car descend slowly until he could distinguish the trees and other prominent features of the landscape. Then he took the steering gear into his own hand and I looked over the side of the car. The forest was thick in parts, but there were wide spaces of treeless plain; and we were just passing over a range of hills which I think I am right in identifying with a range that we had observed at a distance of several miles when we were among the blacks.

I took particular notice of the larger trees, trying to guess their distance each from the other and referring to my watch every few seconds.

"What do you make of it?" said Jack at last, when he had raised the car to its former height.

"It is hard to fix it," said I, "but I cannot think that we are travelling less than twenty-five miles an hour and I should say much more probably thirty."

Wilbraham. Ah! and how far do you suppose that we have to travel from the start?

Easterley. Say fifteen days passed from our parting with Mr. Fetherston until we reached the valley, and I am pretty sure we made an average of thirty miles a day. But of course that was nearly all westing. I don't think that our furthest point could be quite as much as three hundred miles from the wire. I don't think that your own estimate can be much out of the way, but we are perhaps a little under the mark.

Wilbraham. Ah! if the figures are right the sum is easy; we ought to cross the wire about six o'clock.

Easterley. Yes, but look here; thirty miles an hour is possibly an overestimate of our speed; and three hundred miles is possibly an underestimate of our distance. Besides, we shall not be able to keep up our present speed. The wind is already falling, and may be against us in an hour or two. That would knock, say, ten miles an hour off the rate of speed at which we are now travelling.

Wilbraham. It might, but that is another overestimate; we may fairly reckon on travelling all night at within five miles of our present rate of speed.

Easterley. I suppose so. Nevertheless, the chances are that if we stop the car about sunrise we shall still be west of the wire. Then we can lower the car, move north, and watch for the wire, then go slowly, still eastward, keeping a sharp look-out as we go.

We were now both very tired, and as there were still some hours to pass before we could expect to get sight of the wire, we agreed to divide the time till dawn into half-hour watches. Each of us wished the other to take the first rest, and so we had to settle the dispute by lot. I told Jack to hide some lozenges, and to let me guess odd or even. Jack won, but our mode of settling the question was not without important effects. For Jack said, when he was putting back the lozenges into his pocket, "By-the-way, I may as well put these with the others in the car pocket," and he did so.

When my turn came I lay down on the floor of the car, as Jack had done, with my hat for a pillow. The lozenges in my pocket were a little in my way; not much, but just enough to remind me of what Jack had done. Still, I didn't rise, only turned over. Then some of the lozenges rolled out of my pocket. Then I jumped up, and said, "I may as well put mine with yours." I did so, and lay down again and slept.

So now we had all our eggs in one basket, and it never occurred to us that we were incurring any risk at all.

It was eleven o'clock when Jack lay down for his first sleep, and we took regular half-hour turns until five o'clock, when my sixth half-hour was up. It was now dawn, and the light was increasing rapidly. We had had enough rest, and it was getting near sunrise. It was time to think of lowering the car and reconnoitring. The morning was very fine, but there was rather a heavy bank of clouds in the east where the sun was rising. We lowered the car a little, and slackened our speed. Presently we disconnected the battery, and so stopped the car. Then we rested at about four to five hundred feet from the ground. I swept the whole field of sight with the car's glasses in search of the wire, but could find no trace of it. Then I looked westward long and anxiously, but could see nothing

118

specially worthy of notice. At last I fell to admiring the beauty of the clouds; they were beginning to reflect the glory of the sun which was now risen, but still hidden by them. There was in the air that sort of shimmering which portends a dry, hot day. I picked out a small bank of clouds to the west, on the near side of which the shimmering which I have mentioned appeared to be greater than elsewhere. I was quietly speculating on the cause of this when the sun extricated himself from the clouds to the eastward, and his rays fell straight and full upon the clouds to westward. Then I saw strike upon the cloud upon which I had been gazing two shadows which I recognised with horror. I cried out to Jack to look, and I lifted the glasses which were in my hand and turned them to the shadows on the cloud, and I saw that he did the same with his glasses. You will remember that we were now at rest, excepting for the motion caused by the breeze which had almost ceased to blow.

The sun was now shining brightly, and we could make out two dark masses moving towards us. I suppose we ought to have got in motion again as quickly as possible, although I doubt if it would have made any difference at all. At any rate, we did not make the slightest attempt to move, but watched in dead silence the shadows of the contending cars. For that they were somehow contending there could be no doubt at all. The one was trying to block the way of the other, and the other was trying to dodge it. The former was pursuing, and the latter was pursued. The two shadows passed right over us, and as they did, the cars, considering the position of the sun, must have been a little way to the eastward of us; and now it seemed as if the pursuing car was underneath the other, and so nearer to us, and as if the pursued car was being forced upward. Just then, however, the pursued car made a very quick turn westward. The movement was followed by the other car, but it seemed, as it followed, to lose just a little ground. Mind, we could see nothing but shadows, but the shadows were wonderfully distinct. Then the shadows passed over us again, and they were now much nearer, and they quite darkened our car. And now it seemed as if the pursued car had given the other the slip, for it was now the nearer of the two; and then both were straight over our heads. It seemed as if something clashed against us, and we perceived immediately that a missile of some sort had been driven right through the side and floor of our car. It had passed between us, and if it were intended to kill either of us, it had certainly missed its aim. We saw that our car remained steady, and we were too much absorbed in the strife going on above us to notice anything else. Then the same manœuvre seemed to be repeated, for the shadows passed over us again, but this time they were much higher, and the pursuing car was again underneath.

A fourth time the shadows fell across us, but they were still higher this time, and the pursuing car still held its place nearer to us. And now the pursued car seemed to give up the contest, for it held its way westward until we lost all trace of it, and the pursuing car stopped and turned, and came towards us until the shadow was all but over us, and then out of the shadow, as it seemed, there fell a long white streamer. It waved one moment backward and forward, and then disappeared. We swung off our hats together, and gave a lusty cheer.

Then the shadow of the car passed away westward and was lost to sight.

So we had been pursued, and the pursuit was over and our lives were saved. So it seemed, and our joy was great; but it was very soon changed for something very like despair. The car in which we rode had canted over to one side, so that it was becoming difficult either to sit or stand straight in it. We soon saw why.

One of the balloons was slowly collapsing, and on examination we found that it had been slightly grazed by the missile which had passed through the car. It was clear that we must lower the car to the ground as quickly as possible, and it was very doubtful if we could raise it again. A closer examination revealed a far worse loss. The missile in question had been driven straight through the wall-bag which held our provisions, and nearly all of them had fallen through the hole which had been pierced through the floor of the car. It was surely no chance which had given the missile its precise direction. It was almost incredible skill and altogether diabolical malignity. We thought that our enemy had aimed at our bodies and had missed his aim: he knew better: the purpose of his missile was to cause our miserable death in the wilderness.

Jack put in action the machinery by which the balloons were filled, and endeavoured to trim them so as to act together. But it proved quite impossible to do so. The rent in the injured balloon was increasing slowly under the pressure of the gas, and it was evident that it would very soon be quite useless. Jack sang out to me to connect the batteries and to set the paddles in motion. I did so at once and I soon perceived why I was told to do so. The injured balloon was now collapsing so rapidly that we were in great danger of being upset by the one-sided buoyancy of the car. It was necessary to empty the other balloon as quickly as possible in order to keep the car in such a position that we could keep our seats. And the rapid emptying of the balloons would have dashed us to the ground but for the motion of the paddles. As it was we were half turned over before we reached the ground, and we fell with rather a severe crash but without any serious injury. I managed to gather up a few of the lozenges which were left on the floor of the car, as they were rolling off the car when we were fifty or sixty feet from the ground.

Here we were now in a condition almost as bad as when the blacks left us; quite as bad, indeed, or worse, for although we were now probably much nearer to help than then, we did not know where to look for it, and we had no time to spend in finding it. When we were left alone before, we had plenty of water and the means of procuring food for at least some weeks. Now the doubt was if we could survive the second day unless help should reach us before its close.

Besides we were not now as ready to stand hardships as then. We were then in splendid condition. But the nervous excitement consequent upon the startling experiences of the few days which had intervened since then had heavily told on both of us; and anxiety and broken rest had also had their effect. I was myself much worn, but I saw now, or thought I saw, that Jack was on the very verge of collapsing. He was brave enough and ready enough, and very much more hopeful than I was, but there was a look about his eyes and mouth which alarmed me.

"What do you think now, Jack?" I said.

"Well, it's rather a bad business about the lozenges," he replied, "but as for the car, he has only done what I should have liked to do myself; we are well rid of it."

Easterley. But where's the wire?

Wilbraham. Well, old man, the wire is not five miles off, you may be sure of that: most likely not half so far.

Easterley. Why do you think so?

Wilbraham. Leäfar would never have left unless he knew that we were near enough. Besides, all our calculations look the same way.

Easterley. I wish I could see the situation in the same light. Our calculations are based on guesses, and may easily be fifty or a hundred miles astray. And Leäfar most likely did not know that our car was badly damaged and our food lost. Besides, the other one seemed to be quite satisfied with what he had done; for he sailed straight away. But he has not done much after all if he has only dropped us without hurt within a few miles of the wire.

Wilbraham. Well, not much as it has happened, but he was very near smashing us to pieces, and the spilling of the food was a

121

clever extra touch. He had got to do something, and he had about a minute to do it in, and he did his best, or his worst: and as for sailing away, I take it he was beaten away.

Easterley. I hope you may be right. We must never say die, anyway. But you don't look well, Jack, though you speak so cheerfully.

Wilbraham. I am a bit seedy, I am sure I don't know why, but I daresay it will pass off soon.

Easterley. I suppose we had better push on, we have most of the day before us yet, and we had better take some of the food that is left. But look! what's that?

Wilbraham. A horse, by George! didn't I tell you?

And a horse it was, but its presence proved after all not to be such a very good sign as we supposed. We thought at first that it must belong to some of the telegraph people, but as we drew nearer we saw that it was Jack's own horse which had been abandoned in the bush on account of lameness. Still it was a good sign. Its presence made it much more likely that we were still west of the wire, and we might possibly make use of it for travelling, but above all it seemed as if there must be water near, and that if we stuck to the horse we should find it.

It was quite an easy matter to catch the horse; he had been well broken in, and his ten or twelve days in the bush had not made him at all forget his training. He seemed to recognise us, and we thought at first that his lameness was quite gone.

Then we reckoned up our store of food. We had saved just nine of the lozenges. We resolved now to take three each, reserving three for the evening.

If Jack was right we should hardly have need of them. And yet we might, for the telegraph stations were far apart, and it might be quite beyond our power to walk to the nearest, and we would not know in which direction to travel in order to reach the nearest. But then, as Jack said, if all came to all we should cut the wire, and that would soon bring us help.

The food quite restored me, but I did not think that it had the same good effect on Jack. He was quite cheerful, brave, and hopeful, but still there was undoubtedly something amiss. So I proposed that Jack should have the horse and that I should walk beside him. "I don't mind," he said, "if I have the first ride." And so it was arranged.

But riding even a very tame horse without either saddle or bridle is neither a pleasant nor a quick way of travelling, and besides the horse's lameness came on again as soon as he had weight to carry, and it became clear before long that we could get no good of him that way. I had improvised a sort of halter out of slips cut from our coats, and so when Jack dismounted, we tried to lead the horse; he showed a decided tendency, both when ridden and led, to go north. "Let him have his way," Jack said, "provided he doesn't make any westing. I will not go away from the wire." The end of it was that we led the horse, or let him lead us, for several hours. We travelled very slowly, indeed, but still we must have got over twelve or thirteen miles, going mainly northward, and making perhaps a mile of easting all the time.

The country that we travelled over consisted of a series of plains which were separated by thin belts of timber. There was little or no scrub. At last we came, as it seemed, to a small dried-up watercourse; but it proved to be not quite dried up, for the horse trotted over to one of the sand-beds where the ponds had been, and found a little hole of water which he drank very greedily. The hole was so small that we did not care to drink after him if it could be helped; but by digging with our hands in the sand a little higher up we got a sufficient supply of water that was fairly good.

We had now got all out of the horse that we were likely to get. This water meant life for a day or two longer. It seemed now to be the best course for us to start from this point due east. If the wire were even within twenty miles of us we might escape. If not, our death seemed certain.

But Jack's increasing debility, which was beginning to make me very anxious, made it out of the question to go farther to-night. Indeed, it was already getting on for sundown. So we took each, one of our three remaining lozenges, and made our camp as best we could. The trees near the watercourse were shadier than elsewhere, and the weather was mild. We had no tobacco. By some mischance we had left it behind us in our escape from the valley. Indeed, such was our excitement and anxiety that we had never smoked once all the time we were there. But now we missed our pipes very much.

Before going to sleep, however, I made a discovery that cheered us up a little. I found two more lozenges in the corner of my pocket. These would give us a shadow of breakfast.

I slept rather well, but Jack was troubled with restlessness and with dreams. And in the morning he was no better.

Things were looking very black indeed. After making our shadow of breakfast we had but one lozenge left, and then nothing but a little water to live upon. Jack was beginning to show signs of collapse. "I know, old fellow," he said, "that I could not persuade you to abandon me, but I'll die very soon, and after I am dead you will still have time to look for the wire."

"Jack," said I, "look here, shall I go and look for the wire now? I'll come back in two hours whether I find it or not, and then we shall stay together while we live. I daresay we have both of us pretty well done with this world, but while there's life there's hope. What do you say?"

"Well," he said, "I think I can live for more than two hours with the help of this water; yes, old fellow, go and look for it; that's the best chance."

I made him as comfortable as I could near the water under the shade, and then I started with but little hope. I was already getting weak with hunger, although otherwise I was well enough. I crossed the plain eastward to one of the belts of timber I told you of. The distance was about a quarter or a third of a mile. Then I marked a tree, and on passing through the belt of timber, which was only a few yards across, I marked another. I was now in a second plain just like the first. I crossed it slowly to the eastward, came to another belt of timber, and marked another tree.

Then I began to think it was of no use to make any further exertion. Half an hour was already gone; I must in any case turn back in half an hour more. "Oh Leäfar, Leäfar," I said, and I wrung my hand, "how could you leave us in such misery?" And then I remembered how little Leäfar seemed to think of death in comparison with the doom I had escaped, and I was ashamed of myself, and I said—

"The will of God be done."

I had crossed the second belt of timber, and I was marking another tree on the east side of it. I was acting quite mechanically and without conscious purpose, for I had made up my mind to return at once, and so I should not need another marked tree. All in a moment I became conscious of this, and I thought that perhaps my mind was going. Then I turned round to look at the plain which I had just entered, and was just about to leave, and, good heavens! there was the wire! This plain was of about the same dimensions as the other two, and right across it ran the telegraph poles.

I just said, "Thank God," and I ran back as fast as my legs could carry me.

Jack was taking a drink of water, and I thought looking a little brighter. I was quite out of breath, and before I could speak he had time to say—

"Why, Bob, you've hardly been away an hour."

"I have found it!" I cried, "I have found it!"

"Take it easy, man," he said; "take a drink of water. Didn't I tell you we were near it?"

We took near two hours to reach it, for we were both weak for want of food, and Jack was ill. Then we sat down under one of the posts and consulted.

"Jack," said I, "we may die of starvation yet, unless you can cut that wire. I couldn't climb the pole, poor devil that I am, not to save your life and my own."

(You will remember, no doubt, that I have already told you that Jack was a very clever athlete.)

He replied after a silence of a minute or so, letting his words drop slowly: "I should have thought but little of it yesterday morning. I am sure I don't know if I can do it now. I'll try."

"I have one lozenge left," I said; "take it before you try;" and I handed him the lozenge.

"I'll take my share of it," he answered, "but not yours too."

"Now be reasonable, Jack," said I; "my life as well as yours depends on your cutting that wire. If the lozenge helps you to cut it, don't you see that it is best for us both that you should have it."

"Very well," he replied; "I believe you are right; give it me," and he ate it without more ado. And then after feeling for his knife he began to climb.

Presently it became clear that he could not get up the pole without some protection to his knees. I cut off the sleeves of my coat and we slipped them up over his legs; they fitted him so tightly that no fastening was needed.

Then he began to climb again with more success, but such was his weakness that it seemed several times as if he would have to give over the attempt. At last he reached the top, and after hanging for a while to rest he began to cut at the wire.

I watched the process with great anxiety. He gave over several times, and once I thought he was going to faint, and I ran up to the post to try and break his fall. But he began hacking at the wire again, and in a few seconds more it fell apart, and one end of it lay on the ground.

Then he began to slide down the post, and before he was down his arms relaxed their hold, and he almost fell into my arms as I stood underneath.

We both fell to the ground, but without any severe shock, and we were quite unhurt. I staggered to my feet and dragged him to some thick shrubs near at hand, where I propped him up as well as I could manage. He did not quite lose his senses, and I whispered, "We are all right now, Jack; we shall have help soon." Then I lay down beside him.

I do not think that I was more than half an hour lying there

125

when I heard the noise of horses, and in about fifteen minutes more a party of horsemen rode up.

We might have lain there for several hours, however, if it had not been for a combination of favourable circumstances. We were only three miles from a telegraph station to the north, and a sharp look-out had been kept for us. It had been kept indeed since the third or fourth day after our departure, and it had been quickened a few days ago by a lying rumour which proved to be unintentionally true. Some blacks had come into the camp who knew both Gioro and Bomero, and they told Mr. Fetherston that Gioro had been killed some days before. Now, as far as I could make out, Gioro had been killed a day or two after they told the story. So they were certainly lying. But it seemed as if every one who knew anything about the matter expected that Gioro would be killed if Bomero's protection were withdrawn. And so it happened as you have heard, and thus their lie came true.

So there was a bright look-out kept for about fifty miles on each side of the Daly Waters, and a party had gone westward into the bush in search of us a few days before, and the moment the communication by wire was broken a party of horsemen started for the point where the break was made. We were now nearly thirty miles north of the Daly Waters.

We were speedily taken to the nearest station and treated with all the attention that we needed. I needed only food and clothes, but Jack proved to be sickening for colonial fever, and was in rather a critical state for some time. He did not seem to me to be dangerously ill. Much languor and a little wandering and extreme prostration were his principal symptoms. I was not very anxious about him, but Mr. Fetherston thought more of the illness than he chose to say. I did not know the nature of the complaint; I have learnt better since then.

Mr. Fetherston asked me several questions, and I told him all about the blacks, dwelling especially on Bomero's panic and Gioro's death. Then I said that after that we had got among some people that had given us food and clothes. He looked very carefully at the coats and hats, and he said, "Why, these must have come from Java, or perhaps from the Philippines. I had no idea that there was any communication."

I said that I was inclined to believe that the people I had met were not of the same race as the blacks, their colour was much lighter, I said, and they had some curious knowledge.

Mr. Fetherston looked at me with some anxiety and suspicion, and the same evening I heard him say to Tim Blundell that people who wandered among the blacks often got off their heads for a while.

After that I held my peace.

In about six weeks Jack was able to travel, and Mr. Fetherston gave us an escort to Port Darwin.

After about ten days there, we were so fortunate as to get a passage to King George's Sound in a Government steamer. We reached Adelaide about the first week in September.

CONCLUSION

My story is told now, and there is no occasion to detain you much longer. Our life ever since we came back to Adelaide, until the visit to Gippsland which led to the writing of this book, was all of a piece. It was all spent in Australia and Tasmania. We did some squatting, and we just glanced at agricultural and mining life. In every year we spent some weeks in town, and we made some acquaintance everywhere. But we settled down to nothing. We became very little richer, but no poorer. We seldom talked about our adventures to each other, and never to anyone else. But I think they were always more or less in our minds and kept us unsettled.

Sometimes when we seemed to be forgetting them, or when their effect upon us appeared to be passing away, something or other would happen to revive their memory and unsettle us again.

Once, for instance, I was in Sydney with Jack making arrangements for the purchase of a share in a small station. I was dining out one evening on the North Shore and as it chanced Jack was not with me. There was a physician of the company who was a clever talker, and after the ladies had gone away we got him to tell us some of his Australian experiences, which were curious and varied. He told us among other things that he was employed by Government to make a report on some cases in Tarban Creek Lunatic Asylum. After he had examined these cases the superintendent of the asylum said,

"By the bye, doctor, I have a queer fellow here that I sometimes think ought not to be here at all. He is an interesting fellow, too, and I should be much obliged if you would have a look at him."

"I did have a look at him," said the physician, "and I found him just a steady old bush hand, with an uncommon degree of intelligence and good sense, and a lot of information about the country and the aborigines. I was just wondering what on earth they could have sent him here for when he told me with the gravest face the following story:—He had been more than a year among the blacks and he did not know how he was to get back to his own people. It was away in the north-west somewhere, the far north-west. Well, one day, he said, there was a sort of panic among the blacks, he didn't know the cause of it, and he wandered away a mile or two from the camp. He said that when these panics take them

128

they are jealous of the presence of strangers. He had a loaded revolver with him.

"There was no sun and he began to think he might lose his way, and so he made up his mind to return to the blacks' camp. Just then he heard a sort of rustle in the air above him, and presently a man, so he said, jumped out of the clouds and caught him by the collar of his coat. He said that this man never touched the ground himself, but tried to lift him off the ground. He drew his revolver and fired.

"Then he said—'Look here, doctor, I'm blest if the fellow didn't turn into bilin' water and then into steam and then into nothin' at all, and while I was wonderin' what in the mischief war the matter with me back he comes again, fust steam, and then bilin' water, and then an ugly tawny-looking beggar, neither nigger nor white man, and makes another grab at me. So I said, Man or devil, have at you again, and I gave him the contents of another barrel, and I'm blest if he didn't go of in a bile again and I took to my heels and ran as I never ran before until I got back to the darkies' camp.' That was his story," said the physician, "and it appears that he was picked up some months later on the headwaters of the Oakover River by some explorers, and so he got round to Adelaide, and thence to Sydney, and so found his way to the asylum."

In answer to further questions the physician said, "I told the superintendent of the asylum that the man was quite sane, or at least sane enough for the purposes of life; that he was no doubt under some strange delusion, but that I had observed that people who had been much among the blacks were liable to such delusions, and that in my opinion he was quite harmless and that it was cruel to keep him shut up in an asylum, and I made a memorandum in the visitors' book to that effect."

I told this story to Jack that night and we went off the very next day to Tarban Creek to look for the man. He had been discharged and was now working as a clerk on a station on the Murrumbidgee. So the superintendent of the asylum told us.

We hurried off to the Murrumbidgee and found the station where he had been employed. It was somewhere near Balranald. But he had gone away to America about six months before, and we could find no means of tracing him. This affair unsettled us again and was indirectly the cause of our letting the negotiation in which we were engaged drift away from us.

But it is now quite a year since we have made a clean breast of it and committed our story to paper, although we have not at the moment of writing made up our minds about its publication. And the effect upon us both has been decidedly good. Jack says we have done better than the Ancient Mariner, for he had to tell his tale over and over again whenever he met a man whose doom it was to hear him; but we have just told our tale once for all and let the doomed ones read it. And now we have actually settled down to business and have become part owners of a station in Queensland and have our homes within ten miles of each other; that is to say we are quite next door neighbours, and I may as well finish by giving you the details of a conversation which passed between myself and Jack only a few months ago.

We were both staying with some friends at a pleasant little place very near a station on the Southern Railway, about thirty miles from Sydney. I say a little place, for it looked so; but when you came to know it well it turned out to be a very big place. There were as many bedrooms as its hospitable owner could fill with guests; and not to speak of dining and drawing-rooms, which were large and airy and very pretty, there were bath-rooms, billiard-rooms, and smoking-rooms without stint.

It was a quiet, unpretending place to look at, but it was really a most luxurious place. There were pictures and books and musical instruments everywhere; and most delightful contrivances, part couch, part hammock, part swing; and hothouse fruits and flowers; and horses of easiest pace if you wanted them, but somehow you seldom did want them. And whenever there were guests there, and that was three parts of the year, there was the best company in all Australia, and as good as there is anywhere in the world.

Just now the broad verandah, which ran along the main front, was covered with banksia roses, jessamine, and woodbine, and between this and the neat wicket-gate, which was the main entrance to this little paradise, were all sorts of spring and early summer flowers.

At the gate Jack and I were standing; he had come up from Sydney about an hour before. And this was what we said:—

Wilbraham. Well, Bob, can you tell me when you are going to be married?

Easterley. I cannot quite say, but it will be soon. Bessie and I have talked it over and she has listened to reason. She promised me that her friend, Violet Fanshawe, shall fix the day, and Violet is coming here to-morrow.

Wilbraham. And you can trust Violet?

Easterley. I think I can.

Wilbraham. Do you know, Bob, I saw Miss Fanshawe yesterday, and we were talking about you. But she didn't seem to know that she was to decide so momentous a question.

Easterley. Perhaps she didn't know.

Wilbraham. Perhaps not; but, Bob, I think I should like, if it could be so arranged, to be married on the same day as you and Bessie.

Easterley. Jack, I am very glad indeed, but I never guessed it, though I did wonder what was taking you to Sydney so often.

Wilbraham. It was not that; it was, in the first place, to leave you and Bessie together; but sure enough it led to that.

Easterley. But who is she? Oh, Jack, I hope we shall not be worse friends after we are married.

Wilbraham (with a knowing smile). Somehow, Bob, I don't think we will.

Easterley. Surely it is not Violet?

Wilbraham. Yes, it's Violet; so she and Bessie may as well settle both days in one.

Easterley. Well, I am very glad; but how is it that Bessie never told me, for surely Violet must have told her.

Wilbraham. No, she didn't. It was only settled yesterday. But there is Bessie on the verandah, and she has just got a letter.

We both went up to her; indeed we had parted from her scarce half an hour ago. I saw that the letter was Violet's writing. "I'll tell you," I said, "what's in that letter, Bessie. Violet is going to marry Jack."

It was very sudden, and she turned pale and red and then opened the letter. Then, after a few seconds, she cried, "Oh, Bob, I'm so glad!" and she kissed me, and I think she was very near kissing Jack.

So Violet came the next day and the conclave was held and the day was fixed, and just four weeks later Jack and Violet, Bessie and I, were married at All Saints, St. Kilda, for Bessie and Violet were Victorian girls and lived near Melbourne.

And now, as I have already told you, we are living in Queensland, in homes only ten miles apart.

I thought you might like just a little bit of human interest after so much of the other thing.

So now—Farewell!

THE END

131